6P . Level 3.8

Don't Talk to Me About the War

Don't Talk to Me About the War

DAVID A. ADLER

VIKING

VIKING
Published by Penguin Group
Penguin Young Readers Group, 345 Hudson Street, New York, New York 10014, U.S.A.
Penguin Group (Canada), 90 Eglinton Avenue East, Suite 700, Toronto, Ontario,
Canada M4P 2Y3 (a division of Pearson Penguin Canada Inc.)
Penguin Books Ltd, 80 Strand, London WC2R 0RL, England
Penguin Ireland, 25 St Stephen's Green, Dublin 2, Ireland
(a division of Penguin Books Ltd)
Penguin Group (Australia), 250 Camberwell Road, Camberwell, Victoria 3124, Australia
(a division of Pearson Australia Group Pty Ltd)
Penguin Books India Pvt Ltd, 11 Community Centre, Panchsheel Park,
New Delhi – 110 017, India
Penguin Group (NZ), 67 Apollo Drive, Rosedale, North Shore 0632, New Zealand
(a division of Pearson New Zealand Ltd.)
Penguin Books (South Africa) (Pty) Ltd, 24 Sturdee Avenue, Rosebank,
Johannesburg 2196, South Africa

Penguin Books Ltd, Registered Offices: 80 Strand, London WC2R 0RL, England

First published in 2008 by Viking, a division of Penguin Young Readers Group

1   3   5   7   9   10   8   6   4   2

LIBRARY OF CONGRESS CATALOGING-IN-PUBLICATION DATA
Adler, David A.
Don't talk to me about the war / by David A. Adler with decorations by the author.
p.   cm.
Summary: In 1940, thirteen-year-old Tommy's routine of school, playing stickball in his
Bronx, New York, neighborhood, talking with his friend Beth, and listening to Dodgers games
on the radio changes as his mother's illness and his increasing awareness of the war in Europe
transform his world.
ISBN 978-0-670-06307-9 (hardcover)
1. World War, 1939–1945—Juvenile fiction. [1. World War, 1939–1945—Fiction.
2. Friendship—Fiction. 3. Family life—Bronx (New York, N.Y.)—Fiction. 4. Multiple
sclerosis—Fiction. 5. Schools—Fiction. 6. Bronx (New York, N.Y.)—History—20th century—
Fiction.] I. Title. II. Title: Do not talk to me about the war.
PZ7.A2615Don 2003
[Fic]—dc22
2007017889

Printed in U.S.A.   Set in Berling   Book design by Nancy Brennan

FOR MY FAMILY

THANK YOU, Dr. Joseph Straus and Margaret O'Keefe, for talking to me about your mothers' illnesses and treatment; Dr. Joseph C. Yellin, a neurologist, for consulting with me on Mrs. Duncan's medical issues and sharing with me your collection of 1940s medical texts; Amy Berkower and Jodi Reamer, my agents, for your enthusiasm and continued encouragement; and Anne Rivers Gunton, my editor, for your patience, sage suggestions, and constant good cheer. —D.A.A.

Contents

■ ■ ■

1

Don't Talk to Me

Don't talk to me about the war. It's across the ocean, and I haven't even been to Long Island and that's just over the bridge. What I mean is, the war's so far away and we're not even in it. And anyway, it's all Beth talks about, so if there's any war stuff I should know, she'll tell me.

Beth and I meet at Goldman's, a coffee shop that's just three blocks from my building. She goes there for breakfast and the newspapers she loves to read. We meet and we walk together to school.

This morning Mom is standing by the window of our apartment. "Tommy," she says, "wear your jacket. It's chilly."

Mom is holding on to the windowsill. She's a

small, pretty woman with brown hair and blue eyes. I look at her hands. They're steady, not like last night. I say good-bye to her, take my jacket, go down two flights of stairs and out.

Mom was right. It's chilly for the end of May. The sidewalk is crowded with people on their way to school and work, and most everyone is wearing a sweater or jacket.

I stop outside the coffee shop and look in. There's Beth at her regular corner table surrounded by open newspapers. Sitting with her is Mr. Simmons, an old man with a gray felt hat tilted back on his head.

"Hey, Tommy. Did you see this?" Beth asks when I get to her table. She points to a headline: ALLIES TRAPPED! NAZIS AT CHANNEL!

She knows I haven't seen it. We don't get a paper at home. I tell her, "I see it now."

The Allies are the good guys—the English, French, Belgians, and some others. Beth is always worried about them. She thinks the people they're fighting, the German Nazis, are evil.

I turn the paper to the back. BROOKLYN BEATS CUBS, 4–3!

"Look," I say. "The Dodgers won."

I already know about the game. Last night I listened to Stan Lomax and his sports report. Van

Lingle Mungo, my favorite Dodger—I just love his name—pitched five scoreless innings. Dolph Camilli got the winning hit, a single in the ninth.

Beth turns the paper to the front page and gives me that *Don't be such a child* look. We're both in the seventh grade, but Beth is fourteen, almost a full year older than me.

"Do you know what this means?"

She's talking about the war. Mostly I don't understand what's going on in Europe, beyond that they're fighting.

"Sure," I tell her. "It means the Dodgers are just one game out of first. Nineteen forty might be our year."

"The Allies are trapped by the English Channel," she says. "The Germans are headed to Paris and it looks like they'll invade England."

"They're out to conquer all of Europe," Mr. Simmons says. He lifts the coffee cup off the paper he's reading, *The New York Times*, turns to an inside page, and tells Beth, "It says here, there may be as many as one million men trapped."

Beth leans over and looks at the article.

Before she moved here, Beth lived in Buffalo. That's upstate New York, right near Niagara Falls and the Canadian border. "It gets real cold there,"

Beth told me. "In the winter, when Mom was sick, we couldn't leave the house, so every morning we read the newspaper. That was her way of getting out. And she was always real interested in what was going on in the world."

Her mom died, but every morning Beth still reads the news. She says it helps her feel connected with her mom.

Beth lost a year of school taking care of her mom. But she said she was glad she did it.

"The Germans have divided the entire French Ninth Army," Mr. Simmons says, and points to his paper.

"Come on," I tell Beth. "We should go."

"No, really," Mr. Simmons says. "You should read this."

"It's late," I tell him.

Beth finishes her glass of milk.

"Okay," I say. "Now let's put the papers back, we've got to get to school."

Mr. Simmons looks right at me and says, "That's what's wrong with children today. You just don't read."

"I *do* read! I read the sports pages. That's reading. And the baseball games are happening right here, not in Europe."

"Maybe you're right," Mr. Simmons tells me. "Maybe you do read. I just think you should know more about what's happening outside the Bronx, New York."

"Yeah, okay," I say.

"Bye," Beth and I tell Mr. Simmons, but he doesn't answer. He's already looking at another story about the war.

Beth has the *Tribune*, *Times*, *News*, and *Mirror* on the table. We carefully fold them. As we leave, Beth puts the papers on the bench in front.

Soon after Beth's mom died, her dad lost his job. "It's just as well," he said. "Now we can move." He thought a new place would be good for them, would give them a fresh start.

Now they live in the Bronx, and Beth's dad works nights in the press room of a newspaper, the *Daily Mirror*. He gets home about ten each morning, after Beth leaves for school. That's why she goes to Goldman's for breakfast. She doesn't like to eat alone, and like I said, she loves to read newspapers. Mr. Goldman said she can read as many as she wants for free. She just shouldn't spill anything on them, and when she's done, she should fold the papers neatly and put them back on the bench just outside the door.

"What's with Mr. Simmons?" I ask.

"Oh, he says that kids today don't value education. He told me we should think of ourselves not just as citizens of New York, but of the world."

"I don't know about that citizen stuff," I say, "but he's right about school. I surely don't value that. It's boring."

Next door to Goldman's is a bakery. "BAG LUNCHES 15¢," is the sign in the window. Beyond it is a fruit and vegetable store and a shoe repair shop and a newsie holding up a newspaper and shouting the headline. He's just outside the steps to the train station at the corner. It's a busy street.

"The war news is terrible," Beth says as we walk toward the corner. "This could be the end of France and maybe the end of England."

It does sound serious.

"Mom knew it," Beth says. "Two years ago, when the Germans marched into Austria, she said there'd be trouble."

"Sarah lived in Austria."

"Yes," Beth says. "She was lucky to get out."

Sarah came here just a few months ago, and became friends with Beth. Now, every morning, we meet her at the corner. We eat lunch with her, too, along with my friends Roger and Charles.

"One million soldiers trapped!" the newsie calls out as we walk past. "Read all about it!"

Beth stops, turns to me and asks, "Do you know how many one million soldiers are?"

Sure, I do. It's one million.

"The Nazis said this is it," Beth says, "the beginning of the end for the British, French, and Belgians."

"But we're safe here," I say.

"Is that all you worry about?"

I don't answer, but I think Beth should stop reading newspapers. It gets her too upset.

This morning I really want to talk to her about my mother. I'm worried about her. But Beth is only thinking about the war.

Last night it seemed like Mom was somewhere else. Dad talked on and on at dinner, but she wasn't listening. She looked at her hands, so I did, too. Her right hand was trembling, and Mom just watched it, like it belonged to someone else. Then she dropped it to her lap and looked at Dad.

"Come on," I tell Beth. "We'll be late."

We get to the corner. The light is green and lots of people are crossing, but Beth insists we wait for Sarah.

Honk! Honk!

An old Ford, one of those boxy black cars, is

stopped at the corner, stalled, and the people in cars behind it don't like waiting.

Honk! Honk!

I know how those drivers feel. I also don't like waiting. I look around the corner for Sarah, but I don't see her.

"Let's go," I tell Beth.

"Not yet."

Sarah came here from Mexico, and before that she lived in Holland, Austria, and Germany. Beth told me, "She was chased out of Europe by the Nazis."

While we wait, I look at Beth with her books held against her chest and her arms folded over them. She looks different today, older somehow. I know it isn't the dress. I've seen it before. And it isn't her long blonde hair. That's parted in the middle with a barrette on each side, like always. Maybe it's all that responsibility. She does the food shopping and makes dinner for herself and her dad. That probably does something to a fourteen-year-old.

Beth turns to look for Sarah, and I know what it is. Earrings. Gold dangling earrings like the ones Mom wears when she dresses fancy. That's why Beth looks different—older, too, and even prettier.

"There she is," Beth says, and waves to Sarah.

Sarah runs to us with her big leather briefcase. The light changes, and we cross the street and join the crowd of kids going to West Bronx Junior High. And do you know what? Walking with two girls feels good, especially when one of them is wearing earrings.

2

I Might Call Myself O. Tommy

While we walk, Beth tells Sarah about the trouble in France and the trapped soldiers.

"This is very bad," Sarah says. "People I know want to go to France. They want to be safe."

As soon as Sarah starts talking you know she's from some other country. It's not the words, but the way she says them, her accent.

We keep walking and they keep talking, and the closer we get to school, the more crowded the sidewalk becomes. And then there it is, an old big brick building with a bunch of wide steps, maybe eight, leading to real high wood doors.

"Hey, Tommy!"

It's my friend Roger. He stops right in front of

Beth, sticks out his stomach, puts his hands behind his back, and asks, "Who am I?"

"You're Roger," Beth tells him, "and we have to get into school."

"No, no," Roger says. Then in a loud deep voice, "Sit straight. Walk tall. Tuck in that shirt. Now, who am I?"

"Okay," I say. "You're Dr. Johnson."

He's the principal, and he's real big on following rules.

"Are you neat? Are you ready to learn?" Roger asks in his phony deep voice. Then he looks us over, but mostly he looks at Beth. I think he likes her.

"Okay," Roger says. "Now go to class."

Sometimes Roger just tries too hard.

We walk into school and there he is, Dr. Johnson, in his suit and the vest he always seems ready to pop out of, and a tie and polished shoes, just like every morning. He's a tall man, so he looks down at us as we walk by.

"Good morning, sir," Roger tells him.

Dr. Johnson looks at Roger, nods, and watches him walk past.

Beth and I are in the same homeroom, but Sarah and Roger aren't. So we say good-bye to them in the hall.

Our lockers are just outside homeroom. Beth and I put our lunch bags away, take out the books we need, and go to class. Mr. Weils tells us to be seated. "I'm just about to take attendance."

Weils is a rules man, too, just like Dr. Johnson, and a vest-wearer, and about the same age. I'm glad I just have Weils for homeroom and not real classes, because he talks in such a monotone. He's a science teacher, and his classes must be real boring.

The bell rings, and he reads off our names. "Donner . . . Dorf . . . Dorfman." After he calls each name, he looks to see if that student is here and has raised his hand.

"Doyle."

Beth raises her hand. That's her name, Beth Doyle.

"Dropkin . . . Duncan."

I raise my hand. I'm Tommy Duncan.

Homeroom ends and we go to class, and all three morning classes go by real slow. In math, Mrs. Dillon goes over geometric proofs that are real easy, mostly logic. Science, except for the experiments, is a bore, and the American history stuff is all in the book.

A few times during class, I look at my hands and wonder what would make them shake like Mom's. During math I hold one hand just over my notebook and watch it. It's steady. I look at Mrs. Dillon's hands. She's about Mom's age. She's talking about two isosceles triangles, how you know if they're congruent—the same. Mrs. Dillon is sitting on the edge of her desk with her hands on her lap, and they're still.

At least lunch is fun. I sit with Roger and Charles. Beth and Sarah sit with me. That may be a strange way to say it, but that's the way it is. I'm the one in the middle.

Roger, Charles, and I have been good friends since second grade, when we were in the same class. Roger is always joking. Charles is quiet, more sensitive. He's nicer.

They look real different, too. Roger is tall and skinny with dark brown hair and brown eyes. Charles is shorter, chunky, and has short curly blond hair. I'm thin, but not as skinny as Roger, and not as tall. I have straight, light brown hair and blue eyes.

At the beginning of this school year, I brought Beth to our table. Later, Beth brought Sarah.

Roger is always the first of us in the cafeteria, and he gets us a table near the front. We're one of the only "mixed" tables—you know, boys and girls—and both our girls are pretty, Beth with long blonde hair and Sarah with dark hair and eyes. I know lots of boys walk by and wonder how we get to sit with them.

"Hey," Roger asks the girls when they sit down, "did you hear Bob Hope? He was funny."

"No," Beth answers.

Sarah just shakes her head.

"So what did you listen to?"

"News," Beth tells him. "You know there's a war."

"Not here there isn't," Roger says. "We're not fighting anyone. Why should we?"

My mom and dad agree. They don't want us in any war.

"Well, if you didn't hear Hope," Roger says, "you didn't hear this joke. They were talking about who has the most fans and Crosby said, 'When it comes to figures, I've got it all over you.' 'Oh, yeah,' Hope told him, 'if you take off that girdle, you'll have it all over everything.'"

"That's funny," Beth says, and smiles.

Sarah smiles, too.

"Tonight and tomorrow," Roger says, "you should tune in to WEAF at nine o'clock. Tonight it's Fred Allen. You'll like him. He jokes about the news. And tomorrow it's *Good News of 1940*. Listen for Baby Snooks. She's such a brat."

I'm almost done eating. At last, Roger unwraps his sandwich.

"Salami. *Yuck!* I hate salami. What do you have?"

"Egg salad," I tell him. "And I ate it."

Roger always asks what we have, but we never trade.

He hurries, eats his sandwich, and finishes just as the bell sounds. We are about to leave the lunch-room when he tells Beth and Sarah, "Now don't forget, WEAF at nine."

I go to English next, to Miss Heller's class. She stands in front with her arms folded. You should have been here the first day of school. She stood there and didn't say anything. We talked and talked. Finally, we realized she was waiting for us, and got quiet.

"You're in seventh grade now," she said. "I shouldn't have to tell you that when you come in here you should be ready to learn."

Today, Miss Heller is holding yesterday's paragraphs. The one I wrote is about the parachute jump at the World's Fair.

"Your stories were very good," Miss Heller says, and reads from one of the papers. "Listen to this. 'When you go to the Fair, look for the tall red post and the big red, green, and yellow LifeSaver candies.'"

Hey! That's mine!

"'The ride cost forty cents, but it's worth it,'" Miss Heller reads. "'Take a seat beneath a parachute. Make sure to get strapped in. Then up you go! Up!

Up! Up past the LifeSavers. You go two hundred and fifty feet in the air. Don't be scared. Look around at the fair and at the tiny people below. Now hold on! The ride down is fast. *Whoosh!* That was fun. It's a great ride and you should try it if you don't mind waiting in line. I waited half an hour.'"

Miss Heller looks up. "Wasn't that great?" she asks. "I could almost feel the excitement of the drop."

That's exactly what I was trying to do. You know, I think writing should do more than list facts or tell a story. It should make people *feel* something.

Sometimes I think I'd like to be a sportswriter and not just report which team won but write so readers feel the excitement of the game. Imagine that! Part of my job would be going to baseball games.

I like Miss Heller's class. Around Thanksgiving she read her favorite story to the class, "The Ransom of Red Chief," about some crooks who steal a boy named Johnny and send a note telling his parents they will only give Johnny back if they pay a ransom. She said, "Listen to this!" lots of times when she read about Johnny, who is a real brat, something like Baby Snooks. It's the crooks who end up paying the ransom. How about that! They pay the parents two hundred and fifty dollars just to get rid of Johnny.

It's a great story.

The ransom story is by O. Henry, but his real name was William Sidney Porter. O. Henry is his pen name. If I become a writer I might call myself O. Tommy.

After school, Beth, Sarah, and I meet by the oak tree. It's right in front, just down the walk from those big doors. When I get out, Sarah is standing there with her leather briefcase and probably all her books.

"You can't need all that for homework," I say, and point to her bag. "Why don't you leave some books in your locker?"

Sarah shakes her head.

"I'm just taking three books home."

Mine are held together with a large elastic band.

"No," Sarah says, and shakes her head again. "The authorities make searches. They can put something wrong in my book and say I was the person who wrote it."

Beth joins us and I tell her what Sarah said. She puts her hand on Sarah's shoulder and softly tells her, "That doesn't happen here. You don't have to be afraid."

I wonder if that really happens in Europe, or if Sarah is just paranoid.

Beth says, "We'll wait here for you if you want to put back some books."

Sarah had been holding the handle of her bag with just one hand. Now she grabs it with her other hand, too.

"No," she says. She seems upset.

So we start walking. At the corner we stop. The light is red. Beth smiles. "I'm baking bread, lots of it. Do either of you want some?"

"No," Sarah says. "I can't."

Sarah is Jewish and only eats food that's kosher. I don't know what that means, what kosher is, only that our food isn't.

"I can," I say. "I like end pieces."

While we wait for the light to change Beth says, "I wonder what's happening with all those soldiers. Maybe there'll be some news of them in the afternoon papers."

Sarah says, "When I get home, I will put on the radio. I also want to hear about the soldiers."

The light changes to green and we cross the street. Sarah turns and waves good-bye, and we walk straight ahead.

Beth talks on and on about the war.

"This could be a turning point. The Allies can't

afford to lose all those soldiers. And think about the men."

Mom used to talk like that, on and on. She talked about her favorite radio programs and who she met at the market. But now she talks less, and when she does, her words are sometimes slurred.

"They cut off the British soldiers from the French and Belgians," Beth says. "On the one side of the British are the Germans. On the other side is the English Channel."

I want to tell Beth about Mom and her shaking hand, to ask her about her mother and how she knew she was really sick, but Beth is hard to interrupt.

"I'm stopping at Goldman's," she says. "I *must* find out what happened."

This isn't a good time to talk about Mom, I decide, not when Beth is so worried about trapped soldiers.

"Why don't you do what Sarah does? Why don't you listen to war news on the radio?"

Beth tells me, "I do, but it's not the same. The radio is too quick. It's just headlines without details."

"And anyway," I ask, "why are you so interested in the war? You don't know anyone over there."

We're in front of the bakery. Beth stops and asks, "And why are you so interested in baseball? You don't know any of the players."

Beth's eyebrows are raised. She's waiting for me to answer, but I don't know what to say.

She turns and walks toward Goldman's. She takes each of the different afternoon newspapers from the bench and goes in.

I just stand there.

Maybe Beth is right, I think. Maybe baseball is not important, but then I think, if the Dodgers win today they'll be tied for first place and I do know the players. There's Van Lingle Mungo, Fat Freddy Fitzsimmons, Cookie Lavagetto, Dixie Walker, Dolph Camilli, and Pee Wee Reese. I know them all. And Beth likes that actor Clark Gable, and she doesn't know him!

I look into Goldman's. The shop is empty now. There's just Goldman, who is sitting behind the counter reading a newspaper, and Beth.

Mr. Goldman doesn't seem to mind that his store has become her second home. He's a nice old man.

I wave to Beth. I know she won't see me, but still, I wave to her. Then I turn and start toward home.

3

I'm Worried About Mom

As soon as I enter our apartment I know Mom is having a bad day. Near the door is a large, thick shard of glass. There's a pattern etched in it that I recognize. It's from the vase Mom liked. She must have dropped it, and when she swept up she didn't find this piece. The glass has sharp edges. I carefully pick it up and drop it in the wastebasket.

I go into the parlor and see the back of the large upholstered chair. It's set to face the radio, which is on a table by the wall. Mom is small, so sometimes when she's sitting there, you don't see her from the back.

I walk around the chair, and there she is.

"Hi, Mom."

She looks up. "What did you say?"

She leans forward and turns the radio down.

Mom was listening to one of her shows, her soap operas. Her favorite is *The Romance of Helen Trent*, which begins with "Just because a woman is thirty-five, or more, romance in life need not be over—romance can live in life at thirty-five and after."

Yuck!

"Can I help you with dinner?"

"Yes, that would be nice. Oh, and Milly came by this afternoon." That's her friend Mildred Muir. "She brought cookies and I saved one for you."

Mom holds on to both arms of the big chair and pushes herself up.

I look away. Mom doesn't like it if I watch her struggle. She especially doesn't like it if I hold out my hand to help her.

She has trouble with her legs. They're stiff, she says. That's why it's difficult for her to get out of that big chair. And Mom drops things. It started more than a year ago and at first Dad and I thought maybe she had banged her legs. That's why they got stiff, and maybe she was just clumsy. Then she got better, so we forgot about it. But about two weeks ago, it started again, and now it's worse. Dad thinks it might be serious, that she should see a doctor, but Mom doesn't want to.

Mom sits by the table just outside the kitchen. The kitchen is small with just a sink, a stove, some cabinets, and an icebox. Well, that's what we call it, but it's really a refrigerator. We had a real icebox in our old apartment. Twice a week a man came with a large block of ice. In that apartment, there was always a puddle of water on the kitchen floor.

Mom hands me a large oatmeal raisin cookie, the one she saved, and I notice her hand shaking.

"It's good," I say after I bite into the cookie.

Mom smiles.

"We're having meat loaf, potatoes, and salad," she says.

She's sitting, so that means she wants me to take out the food. I have to pretend there's nothing wrong, that I am just helping because I'm a good son, but I'm not *that* good. Dad told me to look out for Mom, to help her whenever I could.

"How was school?"

"School is school."

But then I tell her that Miss Heller read my paragraph. It was Mom who took me to the World's Fair. We went last summer, which seems like such a long time ago.

I scrub three large potatoes in the sink and put them in a pan.

Mom stays in her seat and I bring her everything she needs. As she prepares dinner, I pretend not to notice that her right hand is shaking. I do most of the cutting for the salad and when we set the table I make sure *I* put out the glasses.

After we're done, Mom goes back to the large easy chair by the radio. I tune to station WEAF for her. It's four o'clock, time for *Backstage Wife* and then *Stella Dallas*.

I go to my room, get on my bed, and do my homework. I don't have a desk. My room is small, with just a bed, a chest of drawers, and a window. No closet. My window has the fire escape, so if something happens, like a fire, I'll be the first one out. Great! I hope there's no fire, but sometimes, in the summer when it's real hot, I sit out there and read.

At dinner, Mom hardly talks, so Dad does. He works in a men's clothing shop and tells us about some fat man who came in today and wanted to buy a suit that was too small for him. "'That's my size,' he said. 'Forty-two short. It's always been my size.'"

Dad smiles.

He has a nice smile. I guess everyone does, but Dad smiles a lot. He's forty-two and not fat at all, with a thin face and lots of brown hair with just a little gray on the side. He wears a suit to work, but as soon as he gets home, he takes off the jacket and tie.

Dad says, "The tailor is fixing the suit, but he told me the man is a perfect forty-six short. 'What we should really do,' the tailor said, 'is take a forty-six and switch the labels, give him the larger suit but with a forty-two label sewed in.'"

While Dad is talking, I look at Mom's hands. They're steady.

After dinner, Dad says he wants to do the dishes with me. "We can talk baseball while we wash," he says. Dad's a Dodgers fan, too, but we don't talk about yesterday's game and Van Lingle Mungo.

"I'm worried about Mom," Dad says. "Last night she told me she couldn't see so well. The vision in her left eye was blurred, but when I told her to see a doctor, she got upset. I think she's scared that he'll say something is seriously wrong."

"She's falling apart," I say.

I'm sorry I said it. It sounds so terrible.

"What does a shaky right hand have to do with her left eye?" I ask.

"Maybe she's just weak," Dad says, "but I don't really know. That's why she should see a doctor."

Dad talks for a while about us being a family, that we have to help one another. While he talks, I think about Beth. Her mom had cancer. I wonder if when her mother got sick, her dad said the same things to her.

Dad says, "I told her to see the doctor for me, because *I'm* nervous. I told her I'm sure nothing is wrong, but I just want a doctor to tell me that."

After the dishes are done, we listen to the news. Mom is in the big chair. She looks fine, but I know she isn't. Dad sits in a smaller chair and I sit on the floor real close to the radio.

The news reporter is about as upset as Beth about the soldiers trapped near the Channel. He wonders what Roosevelt would do if the Germans invade England. "You know," he says, "there's a special bond between Roosevelt and Churchill."

I didn't know that. I'm just glad I don't know any of the trapped soldiers, and that America isn't in the war. I think of Sarah and wonder if she knows any of the soldiers.

At seven we tune to WOR, the Stan Lomax sports report and news of the Dodgers. They won again, 3–1 over the Pittsburgh Pirates. Fat Freddy Fitzsimmons was the pitcher.

"Fitz was in control all the way," Lomax says. "He's a knuckleball pitcher, you know, and this was one of his best games. His pitches floated, fluttered, frustrated, and fooled the Pirates players. Freddy

Fitz gave up only six hits in a game that lasted just ninety-eight minutes, the shortest so far this year at Brooklyn's Ebbets Field."

Fat Freddy is great!

Mom has no interest in baseball, but she stays in the big chair and listens. She's comfortable, and it's so hard for her to get up.

Then, while my parents listen to music, I sit on the floor and read an O. Henry story for Miss Heller, "The Gift of the Magi." It's real good! A husband and wife exchange Christmas gifts, but they're poor, and the wife only has a dollar and some change to buy a gift, so she cuts her beautiful hair and sells it and buys a chain for her husband's pocket watch. And guess what? He sells his watch to buy her fancy combs for her hair, the hair she had cut off!

Later, when I'm in bed and about to fall asleep, I think maybe one day I'll take an afternoon job so I can buy Beth a gift, and she buys me tickets to a Dodgers game, only I can't go because I'm working at the afternoon job. Maybe one day I'll throw fastballs and curves like that Cleveland Indians pitcher Bob Feller, but I'll be doing it for the Brooklyn Dodgers. That's what I'm thinking when I fall asleep.

4

Look for a Bottle

The next morning, the apartment is quiet. Dad's lunch pail is gone, so I know he went to work, and I guess Mom is still sleeping. At breakfast, I'm careful not to make noise. Sometimes, when the water is on full, the pipes bang, so I use just a little to wash my dish and knife.

I hurry out and feel guilty. I tell myself I rushed out so Mom could rest, but I know I didn't want to see her hand shaking or hear her words slur when she tells me about the weather.

As soon as I leave our building I realize I should have looked out the window. It's windy and cool for the end of May. I shiver on my way to Goldman's. When I walk in, I see Beth at the corner table surrounded with newspapers as usual. This time she has the table to herself.

"Where's your jacket?" she asks. "It's cold."

"The sun will come out. It will warm up."

Beth points to a map in her newspaper and tells me, "There's good news! The Allies are fighting back! British bombers hit some of the bridges held by the Germans, and the French sent in more soldiers. Oh, and look at this!" She closes the paper and shows me an article on the front page. "The British government is now going to draft even more men to serve in the army. Their new prime minister, Winston Churchill, says his people will keep fighting till the war is won."

Beth tells me what's happening here, that our Senate has voted to spend millions of dollars for our army and navy.

"Why did they do that? We're not in any war."

"But soon we might be," Beth says, "even if we don't want it. We might be attacked or we might decide to help fight the Germans. We can't let them take over Europe!"

"Why?"

That might sound stupid to Beth, but I really want to know why she's so upset about what's happening thousands of miles away.

"Because the Nazis are evil. That's why. Don't

you know what they did to Sarah, that they chased her and her family from their home? And once they conquer Europe, we might be next."

Beth carefully folds the newspapers.

Dad says fighting in a war often sounds like the right thing to do, until you do it. He was in Europe, in the Great War, and said he was in a muddy ditch most of the time. He was cold, hungry, and scared. He saw people killed.

We leave Goldman's, and I look at Beth. I wonder if she would be so wrapped up in this trapped soldier stuff if her mother was still alive. I bet she would be thinking more about her mom's illness.

As we walk past the bakery I just say it. "I'm worried about Mom."

Beth stops. She turns to me and asks, "Why?"

I tell her about Mom's shaky hand, her blurry vision, and that she drops things.

"What's wrong?"

"We don't know, and we're worried. We want her to go to a doctor, to check her out."

"I remember when my mom first got sick. It took a while for her to decide to see a doctor."

And I know what happened to Beth's mother.

We stop at the corner and Sarah is walking toward us. Beth looks at me. She wants to know if she could talk about Mom in front of her. I shake my head. I don't need everyone knowing what's happening in my house.

Sarah joins us, and Beth tells her that the English and French bombed German-held bridges.

"That is good," Sarah says. "I am happy they are fighting back."

The sidewalk is more and more crowded the closer we get to school. Children are talking, shouting, and laughing.

We walk into the building, and Dr. Johnson is standing there, his chest out, stomach in, and his hands on his hips. He says good morning to us, only it doesn't sound like a greeting. It sounds more like a command, that he orders us to have a good morning.

Yes, sir! I think. *I will have a good morning, sir!*

He was a soldier in the Great War, a sergeant. That's what my friend Charles said. Maybe that's why he stands like that and why he's so big on rules.

Sarah leaves us. She walks to the right, to go to her class, and before we go to the left, Beth whispers to me, "We can talk about your mother later, on the way home if you want."

I nod. I want that, and not just because I like Beth. I need to talk to someone other than Dad about what's happening at home.

Mr. Weils is standing by the door to our homeroom. He stands real straight, too, only he's not near-
ly as tall as Dr. Johnson. I sit in homeroom and think
about all that's going on, about the war, the Dodgers,
and Mom. At first, I don't hear Mr. Weils when he
calls my name.

"Duncan," he says real loud. "Are you here or
not?"

I raise my hand.

"I'm here," I answer.

Weird. He looked at me and asked if I was here. I
bet if I had answered, "No, I'm not here," or had not
said anything, he would have marked me absent.

Mr. Weils reads a memo from Dr. Johnson. "Eating
in the lunchroom is a privilege." I know what's coming next, stuff about not running, making sure we
clean our tables—so I don't listen. Mostly in school,
I don't listen.

During history, I'm thinking about Mom, and
Mr. Baker, my history teacher, asks me some ques-
tion and I don't know what to tell him. I don't even
know what he asked.

"Tommy, try to stay with us," he says.

I try, but he's talking about the Constitutional
Convention, the one in Philadelphia in 1787, and I
guess if I had been there, it would have been real

interesting, but listening to Mr. Baker talk about it is boring.

Beth is in history with me. I look at her. She smiles, and I feel better about sitting in class. The bell rings and we walk together to our lockers to get our lunch bags. Beth doesn't say anything about my not listening in class. I guess she knows what I was thinking about.

We sit at our usual table, and Beth takes something from her bag and gives it to me. It's wrapped in paper. "This is for you. End pieces."

It's the bread Beth baked. She even brought some for Roger and Charles. I taste it, and it's better than what Mom buys from the bakery.

"Thanks," Roger says, and bites into his piece. "Just the way I like it."

"Yes, thanks," Charles says real quiet.

In the afternoon, I have trouble paying attention again, even to Miss Heller in English.

What could be wrong with Mom? I wonder how long it was before Beth knew her mom was really sick.

Later, after school, it's windy and raining. It's hard to really talk, so I go into Goldman's with Beth. We sit by one of the tables and Beth answers all my questions.

"It all happened so quickly to my mother," she says. "There really wasn't anything I could do. There wasn't anything *anyone* could do."

"Did her hands shake? Did her vision get blurry?"

"No, she just got weak," Beth says. "She lost a lot of weight. She hurt."

"Mom never tells us she's hurting," I say, "just that her legs are stiff."

"You just have to hope she goes to a doctor soon, that he says it's nothing serious, that she just needs to take some pill or get more rest or something."

We sit there for a while without talking.

Then Beth looks at me and says, "Don't get angry."

"Why would I get angry?"

"I'm going to say something I've been thinking ever since you told me your mom's hand shakes, that she drops things, and her vision is sometimes blurry."

Beth looks at me, takes a deep breath, and says, "During the day, while you're at school and your dad is at work, she may be drinking. Whiskey or wine. You know, she may have a drinking problem."

"No."

"She's home all day. She's alone."

"No," I tell Beth. "Not my mom."

Goldman brings us each a glass of milk.

"Thanks," Beth says.

I also thank Mr. Goldman, "But I can't pay now," I tell him. "I don't have money with me."

He smiles and says, "Don't worry. No charge."

Beth and I sit quietly and drink the milk. It's real cold, real refreshing.

She puts down her glass. "In Buffalo there was a woman on our block who had a drinking problem, and her hands shook. She would make up all sorts of stories. You could never believe her. She said she was once a silent movie star, and she'd tilt her head to the side and say, 'I was also a fashion model. A prince once proposed marriage to me and I said no.'

"I asked why her hands shook and she leaned in close and whispered, 'Coffee. I drink too much coffee. The caffeine makes me shake.' But you know what? When she was that close to me, I could *smell* the whiskey."

I sit there and try, but I can't imagine Mom in that big chair with a bottle of whiskey.

"Look around," Beth tells me. "Look in the pantry, in the back, behind things. Look for a bottle. Check the trash for an empty."

"You're wrong," I say again.

Goldman comes and takes the empty glasses. We thank him and he smiles. He wipes the table with a towel and goes behind the counter again.

Beth says, "Maybe I *am* wrong. I never met your mom."

"I'll look for bottles, but I know I won't find them. My mom is *not* drinking."

Beth walks with me to the door. She takes an afternoon paper from the bench, *The New York World Telegram*. The rain has mostly stopped. I say goodbye to her and Goldman and hurry home.

When I get upstairs, before I go to our apartment, I look in the incinerator room for empty wine or whiskey bottles. There are none, just lots of old newspapers. I take yesterday's *New York Daily Mirror*, the paper Beth's dad works on. It has a good sports section.

NAZIS TRAP THOUSANDS! is the headline on the front page. I turn the paper over. YANKS WIN WITH 12 HITS is the headline on the back. Beneath that is a picture of Dolph Camilli of the Dodgers at the plate swinging his bat with a caption that says it's the ninth inning and he's getting the game-winning hit in Tuesday's game.

When I enter the parlor, Mom looks up. She'd been sleeping. It's past three and there's music playing on the radio instead of *The Romance of Helen Trent*.

Mom looks at the clock on the side table.

"Oh, my," she says.

I quickly turn the dial to 570, WMCA.

I leave Mom and go to the kitchen. There's nothing in the pantry behind the boxes of cereal and pasta. No bottle. I open the icebox. None in the vegetable bin or on the top shelf behind the milk and water.

I bring Mom a glass of ice water and say, "I thought you might be thirsty."

Mom looks up at me, smiles, and says, "Thank you."

When I set the glass down, I lean close and take a deep breath. Mom doesn't smell of wine or whiskey. Beth is wrong. Mom doesn't have a drinking problem.

But if Mom isn't drinking, what *is* wrong? What's happening to her?

5

Helen Trent and Ma Perkins

I throw my books on my bed and open the *Daily Mirror*. There's a map of France, Belgium, and the English Channel with dotted lines, arrows, and numbers showing where the soldiers are trapped. ALLIES PANIC! is the headline on one of the inside pages. It looks serious.

Hey, I think. Why am I reading this? Why aren't I reading the sports pages?

It's Beth. She's gotten me interested in the war.

I try working on my history homework, but after reading six pages, I can't tell you one thing about it. It's funny how I can read every word of something and not remember any of it.

Back in the parlor, Mom is listening to *Ma Perkins*

and folding the laundry. Ma Perkins is worried about some boy who stole a purse and is in trouble with the police. She's always worried about something! On the radio, in the afternoon, it's one soap opera after another. Problems, problems, problems!

"Tommy, will you help me with the laundry?"

I do, and as I fold the clothes, I notice her hands are steady. When she talks, her words are clear, not slurred. Next, I help her scrape and clean carrots and potatoes for a stew and set the table. Then I see how upset she is.

"It's only a radio program," I say. "Ma Perkins will talk to that boy. He'll decide that crime doesn't pay."

Mom is sitting by the table. She doesn't answer me.

"And don't worry about Helen Trent. She's always falling in love with the wrong man."

"It's not that," Mom tells me.

"Is it your eyes? Are you real tired?"

Mom doesn't answer me.

"Lots of people's eyes hurt," I say. "Lots of people get tired. And people fall and drop things all the time. That doesn't mean they're sick."

That's what I say, but I don't believe it.

Mom tries to smile. She thanks me for helping

and says I should do my homework. I go to my room, but I can't work. I'm too worried about Mom.

Dad comes home about six and I hurry out of my room. He has a bunch of yellow flowers—daisies, I think. He asks Mom how she feels, but she doesn't want to talk about it.

"Then how's Helen?" Dad asks, and smiles.

"She's fine."

That can't be true! Helen Trent is *never* fine. Is Mom lying like that woman in Buffalo? Well, not exactly. Mom didn't say she was a silent movie star.

Dad puts the flowers on the kitchen counter. He opens the cabinet just above the sink and looks for the vase.

"It's not there," I tell him quietly. "It broke."

"Oh," Dad says. He doesn't ask how it broke. I guess he knows.

Dad opens the icebox. There's just a little milk left in the bottle. He pours it in a glass for me. He washes the bottle, puts in the flowers, adds some water, and sets it on the table.

"They're nice," Mom says.

At dinner, I think about Mom and Helen Trent. Mom must like the show because, like Helen, Mom is over thirty-five and doesn't want romance to be over for her, and I don't think it is. Sometimes, when *Symphonic Strings* is on the radio, she and Dad hold hands.

Mom doesn't eat much. Dad asks why, and she tells him she isn't hungry.

After dinner, Mom sits in the easy chair and rests while Dad and I do the dishes. We don't talk. I think Dad feels like me—he doesn't know what to say.

We put the dishes away, and Dad and I go to the parlor to listen to the radio. The war news is good. The British, French, and Belgians are fighting back in what the reporter calls the Battle of Flanders.

Next, there's a report from London.

"Just ten days ago, in his first speech to the British House of Commons as prime minister, Winston Churchill told his nation, 'I have nothing to offer but blood, toil, tears, and sweat.' He said, 'for without victory, there is no survival.' This is a crucial time for Churchill and his people."

I think again about what I heard yesterday, that there's a special bond between President Roosevelt and Churchill and wonder how long we will stay out of the fighting.

Dad says, "Too many people here are out of work. We have to get people jobs before we can even think about another war."

Mom agrees. She tells me, "You're my only child. I don't want you to be a soldier."

I'm sure Beth is right, that we don't want the Germans to take over all of Europe. I'm sure Dad is right, too, that we need jobs here more than we need war. I'm confused about all this. I don't know what we should do. But I don't need to decide. That's up to President Roosevelt and all those people in Washington.

At nine, Dad turns the dial to 660, WEAF, *The Maxwell House Good News Program* with Fanny Brice as Baby Snooks. She's such a brat, but she's funny. Her teacher asks, "If you subtract twenty-five from thirty-seven, what's the difference?" And Snooks answers, "That's what I say. What's the difference?"

It's funnier when you hear her say it on the radio in her squeaky baby voice. I'm sure tomorrow I'll hear all the Snooks jokes again from Roger.

Mom smiles when she listens to Baby Snooks.

I change into pajamas, look again at the *Daily Mirror*, and wonder what part of the newspaper Beth's dad worked on. Lying there, on my bed with the light off and my eyes closed, I picture the map and the dotted lines.

■　　■　　■

The next morning, Mom is sitting by the window. "I looked outside," she tells me. "It's cloudy and might rain, so you should take your jacket."

Mom watches me eat breakfast, a buttered roll and a glass of milk. Then, just as I'm about to get up, she takes my hand. She holds on a bit too tight. I can feel her hand tremble.

"I feel fine today," she says. "Don't worry."

But I do worry.

When I get to Goldman's and Beth sees me, she closes the newspaper she's reading. She doesn't talk to me about the war at all. She asks about Mom.

"I think you're wrong," I say. "I didn't find any bottles, and I smelled Mom's breath. It didn't smell of whiskey."

Beth smiles. "That's good," she says. "I don't mind being wrong."

I help Beth fold the newspapers and tell her how I feel, that I am scared. I just wish Beth had a different family history, that she could say, "Yeah, my mother had the shakes. She was sick, too, but now she's fine."

Sarah is waiting for us at the corner. The light is red.

Sarah steps real close to Beth and says softly, "Yesterday we got a letter. It was from my aunt."

I lean close. I want to hear what Sarah is saying.

"My aunt still does not know where Uncle is. She said it is good we left and that we took Yosef and Moshe."

"Who are Yosef and Moshe?" I ask.

"They're Sarah's cousins," Beth says. "They came here with Sarah and her family."

"Yes," Sarah says. "They are little."

The light is green.

"Where is your uncle?" Beth asks. "What do you think happened to him?"

Sarah shakes her head. She doesn't know.

Sarah starts to cross the street and we follow her. She keeps a step or two ahead of us, I think so we can't see how upset she is. When we get in, Sarah hurries to class.

"What's wrong with her?" I ask.

"Jewish people in Europe are taken away by the Nazis. They disappear."

"Go on," Dr. Johnson tells us. "Go to class."

At our lockers I ask Beth, "What do you mean they disappear?"

"Some come back. Others don't. They're just gone."

"I don't understand."

Beth turns to me. "What don't you understand!"

She's almost scolding me.

"They take people away. All kinds of people. It happens every day."

That's scary, I think, but I don't say it.

We get into homeroom just as the bell rings. We hurry to our seats.

Mr. Weils is standing in the front of the room. He's holding the attendance book.

"Sit straight," he tells us. "Sit tall!"

I sit up as he checks the attendance.

My first two classes, math and science, go by quickly. And for once, history isn't too bad. Mr. Baker talks about Benjamin Franklin, the oldest delegate at the Constitutional Convention. He tells us about Franklin's experiments with electricity, and that Franklin believed fresh air was good for people's health. At night, even in the coldest weather, Franklin left a window open by his bed, and in the morning, he often took what he called an "air bath." He sat naked in his parlor, so his whole body could bathe in air.

I close my eyes and imagine Franklin, an old man with long hair, taking an air bath.

Yuck!

I think about another fat man, about Fat Freddy Fitzsimmons and the Dodgers. I hope this summer I can get to Ebbets Field and watch him pitch.

I know I should be a Yankees fan, because I live in the Bronx and they're a Bronx team, but I'm not. Dad grew up in Brooklyn and has always been a Dodgers fan, and so have I. Roger is, too, but I think for him it's just one more way he can be different from most everybody else. Charles roots for the Yankees.

Finally the bell rings.

Beth and I walk together to the cafeteria, and she asks me if I heard what Mr. Baker said about Franklin's air baths. I surprise her and tell her I did.

At lunch, I wonder if Sarah will say anything else about her aunt and uncle. She doesn't. Mostly she doesn't talk, and when she does, it's usually to Beth. Maybe she feels funny about her accent. Maybe that's why she hardly talks.

I sit, unwrap my sandwich, pick out pieces of onion from my egg salad. Lately, Dad makes my lunch, and he makes it the way he likes it, with too many onions.

Roger stands in front of Beth and tells all the Baby Snooks jokes. He does it in Snooks's pretend baby voice.

"'It's time for bed,' Snooks's father said. He was in a hurry. 'First, tell me a story,'" Roger says in his baby voice. "So this was his story. 'A man bought twelve apples. Ten were good. Too bad. The end.'"

Sarah doesn't laugh.

"Don't you get it?" Roger asks. "Two were bad. Too bad. T-W-O or T-O-O bad."

"English is not her first language," Beth says.

Sarah says, "At home we talk German."

"German!" Roger says a bit too loud. He stands, sticks his right leg out real stiff and goose-steps around the table like the newsreels of German soldiers. *"Achtung!"* he says. *"Achtung! Achtung!"*

Sarah turns away. She looks upset.

Roger sits and shrugs, implying he can't imagine what he did wrong. And I wonder why anyone would get upset by something Roger says. He's always joking.

Beth tells Sarah, "He didn't mean anything by that."

Roger opens his lunch bag, unwraps his sandwich—salami—and takes a bite.

Maybe that's why Sarah doesn't listen much to radio comedies: she doesn't understand them. In her house, they probably listen to music. That's the same in any language.

Beth surprises us. She tells us something, and it's not about the war.

"My dad's boss gave him two tickets to Sunday's Giants game at the Polo Grounds. He's taking me, and I need to know about baseball."

"Wow!" I say. "That's great."

Roger stands and pretends to be holding a baseball bat.

"Pow!" he says and swings. "There it goes! Over the fence! You should see *me* play baseball."

Charles smiles. He's a real baseball fan. He tells Beth, "Going to a game is fun, but don't keep asking your dad questions. That can ruin a game. And also, root for the home team."

"What about the game? What do I need to know about baseball?"

We tell her what to expect at a stadium. She already knows about balls, strikes, outs and innings, and how teams get runs. We tell her about dugouts, umpires, and catcher's signals.

"And there's a scoreboard in the outfield," Charles says, "so you don't have to ask who's winning and what inning it is."

"Don't worry," Beth says, and smiles at him. "I get it. I won't ask lots of questions."

After school, Sarah and I wait under the oak tree for Beth.

"Do you have any idea where your uncle is?" I ask.

Sarah shakes her head. "It's a long time since he was taken."

"Maybe he's a soldier, or he's hiding somewhere."

"Yes," Sarah says. "Maybe."

There's Beth. I wave to her. She smiles when she joins us. "It's Friday," she says. "No school for two days."

We're about to leave when Roger calls to me.

"Stop, Tommy! We need you."

Charles and three other boys—Johnny, Ken, and Bruce, eighth-graders—are with him.

"We're playing stickball and we need you. You're the sixth man."

I turn to Beth and Sarah.

"Okay," Beth says. "I'll see you on Monday."

"Why don't you come?" Roger asks her. "You can watch me play. I'm as good as some of those players you'll see at the Polo Grounds."

"I can't, but thanks."

Roger shrugs and joins the other boys. Before I can follow them, Beth takes my hand and says, "I hope your mother is better. I'm sure she will be."

I watch as Beth and Sarah walk away. I look at my hand. It felt good when Beth held it. Then I hurry and join Roger and the others.

6

The Great Roger Burns

Roger lives on the other side of school, about a ten-minute walk. On the way, he repeats some of the jokes from last night's Baby Snooks show. Charles and I heard it all last night and again at lunch, so we stay back.

We talk about school and baseball for a bit and then Charles says, "On Tuesday I have a math test and I'm having trouble finding the number of degrees in the angles, the length of the sides, things like that."

I'm about to say that's easy, but I realize it's not easy for him. Instead I say, "I'm okay with that stuff. If you want, I could help you. Maybe Monday at lunch."

"What about today after the game? Can you help me then?"

It's Friday and I usually like to forget about school over the weekend, but why not? I have nothing better to do.

"Sure," I say. "After the game."

We stop in front of Johnny's building and he and Bruce go in. They come back a few minutes later with a stickball bat—which is really a sawed-off broomstick—a rubber ball, and a few small bottles of soda, Pepsi and Orange Crush. I love Orange Crush. Johnny gives me a bottle and it's real cold. I open it and take a long drink, and save the rest for later.

Roger gives Charles his books so he can have a catch. Then he and Johnny throw the ball back and forth as we walk. Charles and I, each with one arm holding books and the other holding an open soda bottle, follow Roger, Johnny, Ken, and Bruce.

We're not on a main street with buses going by. It's quiet here with just regular apartment buildings like the one I live in. Some people have an entire house for themselves and their families, but I think it's nice here, especially on these quiet streets.

"Think fast!" Roger says, and throws the ball to me.

Both my hands are full! I can't catch the ball. But

I *can* think fast. I stick up my books and the ball bounces off them right back to Roger.

We get to Roger's block and he takes his things from Charles. He drops his history book right in the middle of the street and says, "This is home plate."

There are just a few buildings on his block and not much traffic. It's a good place to play ball. Charles and I leave our books and jackets on the curb, between two parked cars, a Ford and a Hudson.

We all know the teams and the rules. It's always us against the eighth-graders. Roger always pitches. Charles plays infield and I play outfield.

The rules are easy. You get two swings. A batted ball that hits a car or the curb is foul. A ground ball past the pitcher is a single. With fly balls it depends how far they go. Beyond the pitcher is a single, the first sewer is a double, the hydrant is a triple, and the second sewer is a home run. Of course, if Charles or I catch a fly, it's an out.

I finish my Orange Crush and take my place in the street a long way from Roger's history book.

"Let's go! Let's go!" Roger calls.

Ken stands by the history book with the stick held back, ready to swing.

Roger turns to be sure Charles and I are ready. Then he starts.

"Welcome to Ebbets Field. The great Roger Burns is on the mound," he says, sounding just like Red Barber, the Dodgers' radio announcer. Barber has a bit of a Southern accent and Roger is good at mimicking it. "Ole Roger is really sittin' in the tall cotton, tearin' up the pea patch, winnin' game after game."

"Just throw the ball," Ken shouts.

"The fans are anxious," Roger says.

There are just the six of us, so someone from the team that's up has to catch. This time it's Bruce. He crouches a few feet behind home plate, his hands held open, ready to catch the ball if Ken doesn't swing at it, or if he swings and misses. Roger spins his arms around in an exaggerated pitcher's windup and throws the ball. It goes over Ken's and Bruce's heads. Roger is really not a great pitcher. We usually lose, but Charles and I don't care. We have lots of fun playing.

"Oh, Doctor," Roger says in his Red Barber voice. "That pitch was way too high."

He holds the ball against his chest, looks in at Ken, spins his arms again, and throws. This time it's right over the plate. Ken swings and hits it hard, way over my head.

"Can of corn! Can of corn!" Roger calls, meaning it's an easy ball to catch, but it's not. I turn and run for it but it bounces past the fire hydrant. A triple.

We don't have bases, but we know there's a runner on third.

Ken's team hits the ball hard and gets two singles and another triple. Luckily a few balls are right at us and we catch them. They score three runs in their half of the first inning. Now it's our turn.

I always bat first. Charles crouches behind me, ready to catch the ball.

"Here's Tommy Duncan," Roger calls out. "Duncan is having a great year as the Dodgers' center fielder and lead-off hitter. You remember, the Dodgers signed him right out of Theodore Roosevelt High School."

Roger makes this stuff up, but it sounds good.

Ken pitches for the other team. He doesn't wind up. He just reaches back and throws the ball.

I let the first pitch go. It's a bit low. The next one looks good, and I swing and hit it on the ground right back to Ken for the first out.

Oh well. Even DiMaggio, baseball's best player, has more outs than hits.

Charles is up next and now I'm the catcher. Charles hits the ball on the ground past Ken for a single.

Now Roger is up.

"Here's Roger Burns," he says. "You remember, he was brought here in a trade for Camilli. What a great trade for the Dodgers. Burns's great bat really helps this lineup!"

Charles looks at me and quietly shakes his head, and I know why! First Roger says he's a great pitcher. Now he's a better hitter than Camilli, who had twenty-six home runs last year.

"Here's it is, the first pitch to Burns."

Roger swings and misses.

"What a cut! What a cut! It's a lucky thing for the pigeons flying way out on Bedford Avenue that Burns missed that ball."

That's the street beyond the wall at the Dodgers' Ebbets Field.

Roger swings at the next pitch and hits an easy pop-up to Ken.

"He's going back, back, back. He reaches up and robs Burns of an extra base hit."

That's how the game goes. Lots of noise from Roger and lots of scoring for Johnny, Ken, and Bruce. I make a couple of good plays in the field. For one, I reach over my head and catch the ball with one hand. And I get three hits, but just singles, ground balls past Ken.

I don't usually hit the ball real far. That's because

I'm thin and not real tall. Dad says I'll probably grow a lot during high school like he did. You know what? I'd rather grow now.

We play for more than an hour, seven innings, and then stop. We lose by a lot, eighteen to four. But it was fun.

"Good game," Bruce says.

When we finish playing, we usually sit on the curb and talk. But Charles wants me to go home with him now and explain the math, so that's what we do.

His building is just a block away. We sit in the lobby. Charles pushes two chairs together, and I explain the math to him. We do some problems in the textbook and then I make up some more. After about a half hour he says, "I think I understand it."

Wow! I taught him that stuff! Maybe I could become a math teacher. Of course, I'd have to go to college, and I'm not sure about that. But it did feel good helping Charles. Working with him, I realize I really like this seventh grade math. It's so logical. English with Miss Heller is pretty good, too. I guess, mixed with all the boring stuff I don't listen to in school, there's some good stuff, too.

"Thanks a lot," Charles says. "I'll do some more problems this weekend. Maybe George can help me."

He's Charles's older brother. I've met him a few times, and he's nice and all, but not a great student.

I close my book and get up to leave.

"Do you know what George is planning to do in a few weeks?"

"No," I answer.

"He's graduating high school at the end of June and enlisting in the navy."

I sit again and ask, "Do your parents know?"

"Sure. It was Dad's idea. He said it will make a man of him." Charles pauses and then says, "I'm not too happy about it. I'll miss him, and then, you know, maybe he'll get hurt. Some people think that soon we might be fighting in Europe."

Charles and I talk a bit about the war. I don't tell him, but the only reason I know so much about it is because of Beth. Charles knows about it because at dinner that's mostly what his family talks about. His parents think we should prepare to defend ourselves, get ready to enter the fighting.

"George agrees. That's one reason he's joining the navy, and anyway, he likes water and boats. And he'll get training, maybe for a job he can do when he gets out. He'll also get to travel."

I look at my watch. It's almost five o'clock. "I've got to go," I say.

"Sure, and thanks a lot for helping me."

When I'm at the door I turn and look at Charles. He's still there, in his chair, but he doesn't even see me leave. I guess he's thinking about George. That's a big thing, joining the navy.

On my way home, I pass the school. It's so different now with no kids there, so quiet. I stop for a moment and look at it. The two large front doors are closed now. The shades are all set exactly halfway down. That's how Dr. Johnson wants them, so they look neat from the outside. I stand there and I wonder if Dr. Johnson takes his jacket off when he gets home. Probably not. I bet he sleeps in his suit, with his vest still buttoned, and not in a bed. He just leans against a wall, at attention, with his legs together, and falls asleep. That's what I bet.

7

I Count My Blessings

I enter the lobby of our building and go upstairs. Mom is sitting by the dining table with two of her friends from church, Mildred Muir, who bakes great cakes and cookies, and Denise Taylor. Mrs. Muir is wearing pants. Now, lots of women do, but not Mom or Mrs. Taylor. They only wears dresses and skirts.

"Hi, Tommy," Mrs. Muir says, and puts a large slice of chocolate cake on a plate for me. "Have some cake."

"Thank you."

I take it into the kitchen and pour a glass of milk. I'm sure they're talking about Mom's stiff legs and shaking hand. I try to listen, but I can't. They're whispering.

I finish the cake. It was great. I tell that to Mrs. Muir and go to my room.

At dinner, Mom is in a good mood. This seems to be one of her better days, and she liked having visitors. I wonder how she can seem so steady some days and so shaky on others.

"Denise told me I should see a doctor," Mom says, "but not because she thought there's anything wrong. She said I should do it for both of you, so you don't worry, so I made an appointment."

"I'm glad," Dad says.

"I feel fine now, but you keep telling me to go, so I'm going. I just want him to say there's nothing wrong with me, so then you can stop worrying. I'm going Monday."

"I'll go with you," Dad says.

Mom's appointment is in the morning, at ten o'clock.

After that, we're all in good moods, as if the doctor has already said Mom is okay.

I am glad it's Friday night, so I don't have to go to school tomorrow and can sleep late. Dad always tells me he wants me to go to college, to become more than a clothing salesman. But I can't imagine nine more years of school. That's what it would take to get through eighth grade, high school, and college. Nine more years!

I do homework Saturday morning until I'm too bored to go on. In the afternoon, I tune to the Dodgers game, but there's just music and talk. They're in Philadelphia and the game has been rained out. It's raining here, too, so I don't go out. I just read some old issues of *Sporting News* and a book I have about Babe Ruth.

Sunday morning there's a knock on my door. I look at the clock beside my bed. It's just six thirty! I sit up quickly and ask, "What's wrong?"

"Nothing," Dad says as he comes into my room. "It's just that Mom wants to go to early mass."

I don't even get up this early for school!

Early mass begins at seven. It's for people who work on Sundays and for old people who can't sleep late. We usually go later, at eleven.

We walk to church. It's just a few blocks, but I notice how difficult this is for Mom, how Dad holds on to her, how he helps her up the stairs. The later masses are always crowded, and we know lots of people. At this mass there are maybe twenty people and, like I said, they're mostly old. I don't know any of them. We sit in a back pew.

Father Reilly leads the service. Mom sings along, but when Dad and I kneel for prayer, Mom just leans forward.

When we leave, Father Reilly takes both Mom's hands in his. "Peace be with you," he says. "And how are you, Mrs. Duncan?"

"I count my blessings."

"Please, I'm here for you."

He must have seen how Mom struggled during services. That's why he said that.

At about noon, Dad asks me to get the Sunday newspaper and go to the bakery for kaiser rolls, crumb cake, and a loaf of sliced rye bread. I get the *Sunday News* at Goldman's, but I don't go in. I just take the paper off the bench in front and drop the money in the cup.

The bakery is just a few stores away, and at the door I take a deep breath. It smells like fresh baked bread. I love that smell. I go in and am about to ask for four kaiser rolls when I realize they were probably named after some German kaiser, maybe Kaiser Wilhelm of Germany, the one who started the Great War, the one my dad was in. I hesitate, but you know what, I ask for them anyway. After all, they're just rolls. Then I tell the woman I want bread and crumb cake. I pay her and she gives me the cake box and paper bag with the rolls and bread.

I decide not to go straight home. The sun is out, and it seems a pity to spend another whole day indoors.

There's a small park nearby, just a few benches, a set of swings, some trees, and open space. I walk there and see a young couple gently rocking a baby carriage. I sit on a bench near them.

When I was young Mom took me to this park. She thought the fresh air was good for me and she met her friends here, Mrs. Muir and Mrs. Taylor. They would sit and talk and sometimes go shopping together.

"You were a good baby," Mom has told me lots of times. "You hardly cried, and when you did, I knew something was wrong. You were hungry or soiled."

Soiled means my diaper was full. It's embarrassing when I think of that. Mom changed me right here, in the park.

An old man standing by the open space throws a stick. His dog runs, gets it, and brings it back. And do you know what the man does? He throws the stick again and the dog runs for it. How can the dog keep running after the same stick knowing that as soon as he brings it back, he'll have to run and get it again?

I open the bakery bag and smell the bread and

decide I should go. It's almost time for lunch.

When I get home the table is already set. Mom and Dad have been waiting for me. A bowl of noodles and sauce and a plate of Dad's egg salad are in the middle of the table. Of course, you know what I take: noodles. I have enough of Dad's egg salad during the week. For dessert I have crumb cake.

At two, we tune in to the Dodgers game. They're in Philadelphia and the weather is still bad, but they play anyway. Dad listens with me while Mom rests.

It's a great game! The Dodgers are losing almost from the start but just by one run. Then, in the ninth, they tie it with a sacrifice fly by Camilli and win it in the tenth with Pee Wee Reese's first home run ever. It's his first year with the team.

Later, Mom insists on setting the table and making dinner—to prove to us that she feels better. Dad and I watch as she brings in the plates, in case she stumbles, ready to catch the plates before they hit the floor. She doesn't, but she limps. Her right leg looks stiff.

After dinner, beginning at seven I listen with my parents to the radio, to Jack Benny, Ellery Queen, and *The Charlie McCarthy Show* with Edgar Bergen, a ventriloquist. Then at ten thirty the president is on with one of his "Fireside Chats." I listen to that, too.

"My friends," President Roosevelt starts, "at this moment of sadness throughout most of the world, I want to talk with you about a number of subjects that directly affect the future of the United States."

He's going to talk about the war in Europe. I'm sure of it.

"Tonight over the once peaceful roads of Belgium and France, millions are now moving, running from their homes to escape bombs and shells and fire and machine gunning, without shelter, and almost wholly without food."

I'm on the floor. I move closer to the radio. My parents and I stare at it, like we can see President Roosevelt talking to us.

"Let us sit down together again, you and I, to consider our own pressing problems that confront us."

He talks about Americans who believe what is taking place in Europe is none of our business. "Those who have closed their eyes" to what he calls "the approaching storm" have had a "rude awakening." It seems he really feels that soon we will be at war.

He talks about battleships and gunboats and millions of dollars. He talks about spies and traitors, too. I don't understand it all, but I sit there with my parents and listen.

"Day and night I pray for the restoration of peace

in this mad world of ours," he says. "I know you are praying with me."

When the president is done, Dad says, "It's terrible, what's happening in Europe, but I still think it's not our fight. If we go over there, before you know it, thousands of Americans will be running from bombs and dying. We have to protect our country, not the world. That's what I say."

I tell him, "Maybe the Germans will attack us, you know, after they take over all of Europe. President Roosevelt said the ocean that separates us from the fighting won't protect us."

"Well, so far it has," Dad says.

I usually agree with Dad, but this time, I'm not sure.

President Roosevelt said that millions of people are running from bombs and I always thought of war as something fought among soldiers. I know soldiers are people, but they're people with guns and trained to fight. The people he described, the people on the roads, are probably just like us, like Mom, Dad, and me. I imagine bombs falling and flashes of light in the night as we run from our apartment. Maybe we'd run across the bridge to Long Island.

8

Doctor's Appointment

It's Monday morning, the day we finally find out what's wrong with Mom, and it's scary. What could Mom be thinking now? I bet she's scared, too.

It's quiet outside my room, but I know Dad hasn't gone to work. He's going with Mom to the doctor. Mom and Dad are sitting by the table. They're drinking coffee and talking.

"Good morning," Dad says to me. He's real cheery. "I got up early and went to the bakery. We have fresh rolls."

As I eat the roll, Mom smiles and says, "I feel fine today, but I'm going to the doctor anyway. Dad insists. I'm doing this for him. It's a real waste of two dollars."

Mom and Dad don't say anything else. They just watch me eat. I must have interrupted a private conversation. It's uncomfortable for me, sitting there, knowing they're just waiting for me to leave so they can go on talking. I quickly finish my breakfast.

"It's cloudy," Mom tells me when I get up from the table. "It might rain. Wear your baseball cap and jacket."

"Good luck with the doctor."

On the way out of the apartment I wonder what I meant by "Good luck." Do I want the doctor to tell Mom she's fine? Then why do her hands shake? Why does she sometimes slur her words? If he says nothing is wrong, does it really mean he doesn't know how to help her? I guess I want the doctor to know what's wrong and that it's not serious, that there's some pill Mom can take to make her better.

I look at my watch and realize it's early. I must have really hurried to get out. Mrs. Frank is just ahead of me on the stairs. She's walking her two young girls to school. Mom did that, too, when I was young. She walked with me every morning.

"Margie doesn't play with me at recess," the younger of the two girls tells Mrs. Frank.

"I don't want to play with her," her sister says. "I want to play with my friends."

Charles likes having an older brother. I bet when the Frank girls get older, they'll be glad they have each other. Right now I wish I had a brother or sister I could talk to about Mom.

When I get outside, I see Mom was right. There's a misty drizzle in the air and lots of dark clouds that seem ready to bring real rain.

I close my jacket and put on my light blue Dodgers hat with the large white *B* for Brooklyn in the front, and start toward Goldman's.

A tall young man holding a large open black umbrella is ahead of me. He has on a suit and necktie and is carrying an armload of shirts. When he gets to the cleaners on the next block, he closes his umbrella and walks in. He looks to be just out of high school. If we go to war, he would probably be called to serve and would soon be wearing a uniform. Instead of carrying shirts to the cleaners, he would be carrying a gun into battle.

As he drops his shirts on the counter, I wonder what he thought of the president's speech last night, what he thinks about going to war. For him, war won't be something he'll read about in newspapers. War might be something that will take his life.

Dad once told me that in the Great War he saw men die. Every moment he was in battle he thought he might be next. He still has his uniform. Mom once showed it to me. It's in a box in his closet, but I've never seen Dad put it on or even look at it.

Goldman's is on the next block. It's especially noisy and crowded today, and all the stools by the counter are taken. Most of the seats at the tables are taken, too. I look in and see Beth sitting at the corner table, *her* table. Mr. Simmons is sitting across from her. There are a few newspapers open in front of them and they're talking.

Beth looks up.

"Hi, Tommy. How's your mom?"

"Fine."

I won't tell her about the doctor's appointment with so many people around.

"The war news isn't good. The French lost Boulogne, a port along the English Channel. You know, if the Germans cut off the Channel, the Allied soldiers will be completely trapped."

"Eleanor, the president's wife, was talking to some students," Mr. Simmons tells me. "They're against what we're doing to get ready to fight, and she said, 'I don't want to go to war. But war may come to us.'"

He points to the newspaper again and says, "Look. It's right here."

I just hate it when he tells me to read stuff.

"That's okay," I tell him. "I trust you. I'm sure that's what she said."

He looks up and smiles. "I heard her speak many years ago, when I was in college. I saw her."

"Really? Was she nice?"

"She was radiant," Mr. Simmons says. "Her smile brightens her whole face. It cheers you just to see her."

"That's so great. I'd love to see Mrs. Roosevelt."

"We should go," Beth says. "We don't want to be late."

It's amazing to me that someone I know actually saw the president's wife. But Beth is right. We *should* go.

I say good-bye to Mr. Simmons, and I admit, I'm impressed he went to college. The only people I know who went are my teachers, and I guess Father Reilly.

"He's seen lots of interesting people," Beth tells me as we leave the coffee shop, "gangsters and actors, and once he opened the door for Babe Ruth and he told me Mr. Ruth was real polite."

That reminds me about the baseball game Beth went to. I ask her about it.

"I had fun. It was chilly and there was some rain, but there were lots of home runs—and the Giants won!"

"That's great."

"We had seats upstairs, in the open, but when it started to rain we moved to a covered area. There were lots of empty places. And I did what you and Charles told me to do. I looked at the scoreboard and didn't ask a lot of questions."

We're outside now.

"I wanted to talk to you," I say, "and not in Goldman's, not with all those people around."

I move away from the curb, closer to the repair shop, so people can walk by.

"Mom made an appointment to see a doctor. She's going there this morning. Dad is going with her."

"Oh."

We just stand there for a moment.

"I keep thinking about what horrible disease she might have."

"It's scary," Beth says, "but it's really the best thing, that she sees a doctor. It may be nothing serious and if it is something, the doctor will know what to do."

"You know what worries me the most? It's when I look at Mom. She's the only one who really knows how she feels, and she doesn't just look shaky and weak. Lots of times, when I look at her, she looks scared."

"A lot of the time, that's how my mom looked."

"I guess people know when they're sick, when they're *really* sick."

We stand there, near the corner. The newsie is calling out today's headline just like he does every morning. Some people stop and buy a newspaper. Others hurry past him to the train. That's how things go, I guess. No matter what is happening in your life, the world moves on.

I look closely at the newsie for the first time. He looks to be just a year or two older than me. I wonder why he's not on his way to school. Maybe I'll be doing that in two years, selling newspapers to help pay doctor and hospital bills.

"Beth, do you remember the first time your mom went to the doctor? Do you remember what he said, what you did?"

"Yes. At first, the doctor wasn't sure what was wrong with her, but he thought it might be serious. He sent Mom to another doctor. It was the second one who told her it was cancer. We were all terribly upset, but Mom didn't seem surprised. I think, all along, she knew she had some terrible disease."

What is Mom thinking right now? Is she as scared as I am?

Beth says, "The doctor thought he caught it early. We believed she would get better. We hoped she would. She just didn't."

There's nothing I can say.

"She took medicines. She was in and out of the hospital. Nothing seemed to help. She got weaker and weaker and then . . ."

Beth stops.

We stand there for a moment, quiet.

Beth wipes her eyes. "Let's go," she says. "Sarah is probably waiting."

Maybe I shouldn't ask Beth again about her mom. She gets upset when she talks about her—and really, so do I.

Sarah is standing by the corner with her over-stuffed book bag.

"I thought maybe you were not coming," Sarah says. "We must be very quick."

The light is red. Sarah stares at it and taps her foot. She seems impatient, anxious to get to school.

"Don't worry," Beth tells her. "Nothing will happen if we're a minute or two late."

"No," Sarah says. "We must not be in trouble with the authorities."

Here we don't call the principal and teachers in a school "the authorities," but I guess that's what they are. That just seems so official, so all-powerful.

The traffic light turns green and Sarah quickly crosses the street. We have to rush to keep up with her. The bell rings just as we're walking up the front steps of the school.

Dr. Johnson looks at us disapprovingly as we walk into the building. Sarah has her head down as she walks quickly to the right. Beth and I go to the left.

We hurry, but this doesn't seem important, getting to class on time so Mr. Weils can call out my name and check if I raise my hand.

"You're late," Mr. Weils says when we enter homeroom. "I'm just about to take attendance."

As he calls our names, I think again about Mom. The bell ending homeroom startles me. I walk to math, but I'm mostly in a haze the rest of the morning. I keep looking at my watch. Then, in the middle of science, it's ten o'clock and I know that just then Mom is seeing the doctor.

At ten forty-five the bell rings. Surely by now the doctor has spoken to Mom. He's told her his diagnosis and strangely, even though I don't know what he said, I feel relieved. All through history I tell myself, At least now we know what's wrong.

Beth sits on the other side of the room, by the windows. She often looks over at me during class, to see if I'm paying attention to Mr. Baker. Usually, I'm not. After class, she walks with me to our lockers.

"During history, were you thinking about your Mom?"

"Yes."

"Did you hear Mr. Baker tell us about the test? It's on Wednesday, on chapters twelve and thirteen."

"Oh. Thanks."

We get our lunch bags, go to the cafeteria, and sit with Sarah, Roger, and Charles. I unwrap my sandwich, take off the top slice of bread, and pick out pieces of onion from the egg salad.

Roger asks, "Did you listen to Jack Benny last night and to Charlie McCarthy?"

Sarah shakes her head.

"No," Beth tells him. "We listened to the president."

"Benny and Charlie were on earlier, before the president. But it's okay if you didn't hear them. I'll tell you their best jokes."

While Roger jokes, Beth reaches out and puts her hand on mine. "Don't worry," she whispers. "The doctor will know what's wrong."

Roger stops for a moment. He sees Beth's hand

on mine. I know he wishes it was his hand she was holding. He likes her, too. Charles and Sarah also look.

All through lunch, Roger watches Beth. He wants her to laugh at his jokes. So do I. She has a cute laugh.

The bell rings. We clean up and on the way out, Charles asks, "What was Beth talking about when she told you not to worry?"

"I'll tell you later," I say, but I'm not sure I will.

I *know* I won't tell Roger.

9

One Big Nasty Circle

The rest of the day is a blur. I just think about Mom. She's already left the doctor's office and knows what's wrong. Dad knows, too. They're both either very relieved or very upset. I just hope it's good news.

After my last class I go outside by the oak tree and wait for Beth. Sarah is already there. Since she never goes to her locker to leave her books, she's always the first one out.

Beth is taking longer than usual, or maybe it just seems longer because I'm anxious to get home.

"Tommy," Sarah says softly. "You look sad. Is there something that is wrong?"

"I hope not."

Roger and Charles walk past.

"Don't forget, seven thirty," Roger says, "the Lone Ranger."

Charles waits behind and asks, "Is everything okay?"

Roger has stopped. He's waiting for Charles.

"Yes," I answer. "Everything is fine."

I hope that's true, and anyway, I'm just not ready to get into a long conversation with Charles about Mom and have Roger come over and want to know what we're talking about. Then I'd have to tell them everything that's been happening at our house. I'm just not ready for that. I just want to get home.

"Okay," Charles says, "because if there's a problem or something—you know."

"Okay, thanks."

I must really look worried. First Sarah noticed and now Charles.

There's Beth in a crowd coming down the front steps of the school. It's easy to pick her out, with her long blonde hair and colorful dress. She sees us and smiles. "Sorry I'm late."

We walk quietly. At the corner, after we cross the street, Sarah says, "I hope everything is good."

"Thank you."

Beth and I walk to Goldman's and I stop, but

Beth doesn't. She turns and tells me, "I'm walking home with you so you can tell me what happened at the doctor's office."

"No, you like to read the afternoon papers. You want to know what happened with the soldiers."

"I'll read about them later. Right now I want to know what the doctor said."

Beth has never been to our apartment building. I've never been to hers. From the outside, most buildings in the Bronx look the same—brick, a few stories high with a metal fire escape crawling up each side and usually tablecloths and laundry hanging from a few windows.

"This is it," I say when we come to my building. I open the door for Beth.

Our building doesn't have much furniture in the lobby, just a small table and two large cloth-covered chairs that I think some family left when they moved out. The chairs are worn but comfortable. We walk in and see two old women sitting, talking, and waiting for the mailman who comes in the late afternoon. One of the women, the heavy one, seems to do most of the talking.

"Hello," I say as we walk past.

I always greet them, but I don't know their names and I don't think they know mine. Apartments are funny like that. We live in the same building but once we close our doors, we're each in our own private worlds.

The stairs are at the end of the lobby, on the left. They're wide at the bottom with a curly metal handrail. Beth sits on the second step and says, "I'll wait here."

I'm about to walk up, when Beth says, "Good luck."

"Thanks," I say, and take her hand.

I'm a little scared. I wonder what's waiting for me in *my* private world. I let go of Beth's hand and start up the stairs. When I reach our apartment, I unlock the door and listen. No one calls to me. No one is waiting anxiously for me to come home. Either nothing is wrong with Mom and she's out shopping or celebrating with Dad, or Mom is so sick the doctor is still examining her, or even worse, she was rushed to the hospital.

Mom's raincoat is in the small front closet, so she must be home. I find her resting in the big easy chair. The radio is tuned to soft music, not to her soap operas.

Mom hears me and opens her eyes.

"Tommy, you're home."

"Yes."

"Good. Maybe you'll help me with dinner."

"Sure, Mom."

Mom holds on to both arms of the chair, pushes herself up, and walks stiffly toward the kitchen. I follow her and stop in the dining area, by the table. The kitchen is too small for both of us. Mom takes a pot from the drawer beneath the counter, puts it in the sink, and fills it with water.

"Aren't you going to tell me? What did the doctor say?"

Mom puts the pot on the stove, on one of the burners, and lights it. Then she turns to me.

"He thinks I'm tired."

"That's it! You're just tired?"

Mom nods. "And I might be depressed."

"Depressed! Why? What's wrong?"

"What's wrong! My leg is stiff. My hand shakes. Sometimes my vision is blurry. That's enough to make anyone depressed."

I think about that for a moment, but it doesn't make sense to me. How could being depressed cause all Mom's physical problems if it's the problems that are making her depressed? That's just one big nasty circle.

"But Mom, that doesn't make any sense."

"I know. None of this makes any sense to me.

I've been tired before, but that never gave me the shakes."

The water starts to boil. Mom opens a box of elbow noodles and pours them into the pot.

"I'm making pasta salad. Your father likes that."

"I like it, too."

"And I'm cooking chicken, but I'll do that later. I want it ready about six, when Dad gets home."

Just then I remember that Beth is waiting for me.

"I'll be right back," I say, and hurry out of the apartment.

Beth is still sitting on the second step. She's reading our history book, studying for Wednesday's test. She sees me coming down the stairs, closes the book, and gets up.

I reach the lobby floor, look at Beth a moment and then tell her, "The doctor said Mom's just tired and maybe depressed."

"That's all?"

I nod.

"No disease?"

I shake my head.

"Then that's good news," Beth says, and hugs me. "I'm so happy for you."

I hold on to her and we stand like that for a bit, and then Beth steps back. I see tears in her eyes as she gathers her books. "I'll see you tomorrow," she says.

I wipe my eyes. They're teary, too.

Beth leaves the building and I notice the two old women. They're still sitting in the lobby and they're watching me. I smile at them and then go back upstairs.

Mom is standing by the stove, stirring the noodles. Later, while I help her clean the chicken and make the salad, she describes the doctor and his office. When she and Dad left it, they went to a coffee shop for some ice cream.

"Dad told the man we were celebrating and he brought us each a piece of chocolate cake. 'No charge,' he said."

It must be Goldman's. Mom doesn't know I meet Beth there every morning.

"Dad thinks maybe I'm depressed," Mom says as I squeeze a lemon over the salad, "because of my radio programs. He thinks maybe all Helen Trent's troubles and Ma Perkins's are upsetting me. Dad told me to listen to music instead, so that's what I did this afternoon, but I miss Helen, Mary Noble, and Ma Perkins. It's lonely all afternoon without them."

Lonely without some made-up radio people! Maybe Dad is right. Maybe Mom *is* too wrapped up in those stories. Maybe she should sit in the park with her friends.

"The doctor was nice. He said in winter, with less sun and the cold weather, some people get depressed. He hopes with the coming of summer, I'll be better. He said I shouldn't worry, just get more rest."

We don't talk much after that. Mom drains the water from the pot of noodles and when she sets it on the counter to cool, I notice her right hand still shakes. She goes back to the big chair and I go to my room and do homework.

At dinner, Dad tells Mom everything she should and should not do. He's determined that she not work so hard. He tells her to "think happy thoughts."

While we wash the dishes, Dad tells me, "You can't imagine what I was thinking this morning. I sat in the waiting room with Mom and worried about all the terrible diseases she might have."

Of course, I can imagine that.

After dinner, Dad tunes the radio to Stan Lomax and the sports news.

"New York's three baseball teams won twice today and lost once," Lomax reports. "The Yankees and Dodgers won. The Giants lost."

Yeah!

I look at Mom. She has a faraway look in her eyes,

like she isn't even listening. I don't think she really cares if the Dodgers win or lose, which is too bad. They're really doing great this year. This season, I don't think any Dodgers fans are depressed.

Dad tunes the radio to "old people" slow classical music. I hear enough of that in school, in Music Appreciation! I like swing, the new sound. Sometimes, when I listen to it on the radio, I tap to the beat and not because I want to. I just do. And I never tap to the old stuff my parents like. I go to my room and read some history, but at nine, I'm out again. I want to hear Lux Radio Theater.

Each Monday night it takes a popular movie and makes it into an hour-long radio play, usually with some of the stars from the movie. It always begins with, "Greetings to you from Holly Woooood." That's how the producer of the show, Cecil B. DeMille, says it, like Holly and Wood are two separate words.

After some talk about Lux Flakes, Mr. DeMille says, "And now the curtain goes up on act one of *Vigil in the Night.*"

The first scene is in a hospital. Two sisters are nurses and one of them makes a tragic mistake and a child dies. I look at Dad. This won't help Mom have happy thoughts.

"It's late," Dad says quickly. "I'm turning this off."

He gets up and reaches for the radio.

"No," Mom tells him. "I'm not a child. I can listen to a program about nurses and a hospital. You know I look forward all week to Lux Radio Theater."

Dad sits again. I listen awhile longer. I usually like the Lux show but this one depresses me, not because a child dies, but because it turns into a love story between a doctor and one of the nurses. It's too much like one of Mom's soap operas. At the end of the first act I say good night and go to my room.

What a good day this was! Mom isn't really sick. And it was nice of Beth to walk me home. She seemed worried, too, about Mom, and relieved to know the doctor said she was just tired.

She looked pretty today, in her green dress and earrings. She wears them all the time now. It felt nice to be hugged. Today, I really needed that.

10

Half Blind!

*B*ang!

A noise outside wakes me. It sounded like a car backfiring.

I look at the clock beside my bed and realize I forgot to set the alarm. It's late. I have to hurry. I sit up and see a note taped to the inside of my door.

Please be quiet. Mom is sleeping.

I hope that car didn't wake her.

I skip breakfast and hurry out. I'm anxious to get to Goldman's. Then, as I'm about to enter the coffee shop, a man pushes past me. It's Mr. Simmons. He grabs a *New York Times* from the bench and quickly looks through it. He drops it and grabs a *Herald*

Tribune. He looks at the front page and says real loud, "It's not in here."

People put down their cups of coffee. The shop is suddenly quiet.

"I heard some exciting news, and it's not in the papers."

I slip past him, sit beside Beth at the corner table, and listen.

"They're getting away," he says all excited. "They're getting on boats, all sorts of boats—fishing boats, rowboats, sailboats—and they're getting away."

"Who's getting away?" a woman at the table next to us asks.

"The trapped soldiers. The Allies. It started Sunday night. There's fighting in the air with airplanes shooting it out. Dogfights. And all these boats are taking Allied soldiers across the Channel, from Dunkirk to Dover. It was quiet and steady—an amazing rescue. At first, I don't think the Germans knew what was happening."

People begin to talk. Mr. Simmons drops the *Tribune* on Beth's table and sits next to me.

"It started Sunday night, European time. That's the afternoon here. Now it's Tuesday. There should be something about it in the papers."

Mr. Goldman is standing by our table and asks, "Where did you hear this?"

"On the radio. WEAF, on the half-hour European news program."

Mr. Goldman hurries behind the counter. He tunes his radio to WEAF, turns up the volume, and we hear some man singing.

"No!" a woman calls out. "That's the Gene and Glenn show, a half hour of songs. Try WMCA. They mix news with music."

The woman and others gather by the counter and Mr. Goldman turns the dial to the left. We hear music. It sounds to me like Glenn Miller's band.

I look at my watch.

"Beth, we have to go."

"Wait," she tells me.

Mr. Goldman turns the dial again and finally gets some news. The announcer says, "Reports have been confirmed. In an amazing rescue, thousands of Allied soldiers have escaped capture at Dunkirk."

Beth leaves her seat and gets close to the counter, so I do, too.

"They were transported from the shore at Dunkirk," the announcer says, "across the Channel in an unlikely armada of boats of all kinds."

"Did you hear that?" Beth asks me.

Of course I heard it.

"Right now there are boats waiting on the coast of France to take whatever men can get to them, Allied soldiers who until now seemed lost to the German onslaught. This, while the enemy flies over and drops bombs on the coastline and into the water to stop the withdrawal."

"We really have to go," I tell Beth again. "It'll be in the afternoon papers."

We return to the corner table and fold the newspapers. Beth is especially slow this morning gathering her books. I guess she doesn't want to leave until the bulletin ends.

"The rescue comes along with the disappointing collapse and surrender of Belgium's army. Stay tuned to this station for all the latest news."

Now we can leave.

Beth puts the newspapers on the bench as we walk outside.

"That's the second bit of really good news this week," Beth says. "First your mother and now this."

It does seem to be a good week.

We're in front of the bakery and I hear the newsie call out today's headline about the surrender of Belgium's army and King Leopold's ministers, escape to England. Someone should tell him about the rescue.

We're almost at the corner now and Beth says, "Thursday is Memorial Day. No school. Let's meet at Goldman's at about noon for lunch or ice cream. We'll celebrate."

"Sure."

I look at Beth as we continue walking. She's wearing her white dress with pink and yellow stripes. It's my favorite. Of course, she's wearing earrings, too. These are small silver hoops. They look nice.

Sarah is at the corner waiting for us. I take a few quick steps ahead, so I can tell her my news before Beth tells her about the soldiers. I tell Sarah that Mom seemed to be so sick, that her hand shook, her legs were stiff, and that yesterday she went to the doctor. That's why I looked so worried.

"The doctor said she just needs to rest."

Sarah smiles.

"I am happy for you."

"And listen to this," Beth says, and repeats the news report we heard at Goldman's, almost word for word.

"The soldiers are safe?" Sarah asks.

Beth nods.

"This is very good. It is a victory," Sarah says.

"Well, not really. The Allies didn't defeat the Germans. They just got away."

Sarah has more questions, but Beth can't answer most of them, so after school Sarah will go with her to Goldman's. It's sure to be in the afternoon papers.

We walk up the wide steps and enter school. Dr. Johnson is standing there, as formidable as ever, and I can hardly believe what Beth does. Sarah and I are anxious to get by as quickly as we can, and Beth stops to talk.

"Did you hear the good news?" she asks the principal.

"Move along," Dr. Johnson says. "Go to your homeroom."

He stands there with his chest out and his feet apart, as if his sergeant just said, "At ease, soldier." Dr. Johnson's eyes dart from side to side, checking students as they enter the building.

"The Allied soldiers, the ones trapped by the English Channel, have been rescued."

Dr. Johnson looks down at Beth. There's an odd expression on his face, one I haven't seen before. It's almost a smile.

"How do you know this?"

"I just heard it over the radio."

Beth starts to tell Dr. Johnson what we heard, and he's no longer interested in the children walking by.

"I'm going to class," I tell Beth and Dr. Johnson.

"Yes. Yes," Dr. Johnson says. "Go to class."

I enter our classroom and Mr. Weils tells me to go to my seat. "I'm just about to take attendance."

The bell rings and Mr. Weils starts.

"Donner . . . Dorf . . . Dorfman . . . Doyle."

"She's here," I call out. "She's in the hall talking to Dr. Johnson."

"Are you Beth Doyle?" Mr. Weils asks.

"No. Of course not."

"Is she in this room?"

I shake my head.

"Then she's absent."

Mr. Weils continues with the roll. When he calls out my name, I raise my hand.

The bell rings at the end of homeroom and finally there's Beth with Dr. Johnson. They're standing by the door.

"Don't mark her late," Dr. Johnson tells Mr. Weils. "She was with me."

"Yes, sir," Mr. Weils responds.

I look at Mr. Weils and smile. His right hand is at

his side. The fingers are together and stiff—like he is ready to salute.

Beth and I walk together toward our first-period classes. I have math. She has science.

"Where were you? What happened?"

"He has a radio in his office. We went there and listened to the news."

We are by Mrs. Dillon's room, where I have math. Beth's science class is down the hall.

"You went to Dr. Johnson's office?"

Beth nods. "I'll tell you more later."

She smiles and rushes to her science class. I enter Mrs. Dillon's room and see her by the blackboard drawing triangles and labeling the angles and sides.

During math, I wonder about Beth. What was she thinking when she asked me to meet her on Thursday? Are we just two friends meeting for ice cream or are we more than friends? Will it be a date? Should I pay for both ice creams?

My next class is science, and Mr. Jacobs keeps us late, after the bell rings, so he can finish what he's saying, only I don't know what that is. I'm not really listening. I get to history just before the bell starting third period, too late to talk to Beth. But we do talk after class, on our way to our lockers and the cafeteria.

"Dr. Johnson and I listened to the WHN news report," Beth tells me. "It was the same as the one we heard in Goldman's."

We're just entering the cafeteria.

"You should see his office," she says. "There is a picture of him with his rifle and uniform and another in front of a captured German tank. He looked so different when he was young, so skinny. He had hair and he even smiled in the pictures. On top of one bookcase is a helmet. He told me it's the one he wore in the Great War."

We're by our table now.

I say, "I bet he still has his rifle, maybe even in his office."

Roger asks, "Who has a rifle in his office?"

"No one," I answer, and tell him where Beth was this morning.

"So, you got in trouble again. You were sent to the principal's office," Roger says, and shakes his finger at Beth.

Beth ignores Roger and describes the rescue at Dunkirk. Charles, Sarah, and I listen as Beth talks about the soldiers and the power of the German Army, how it so quickly conquered Poland, Denmark, Norway, and Holland, that it's marching through Belgium and France. She describes the amazing rescue. I don't think Roger is real interested, but he listens, too.

After school, I walk with Beth and Sarah to Goldman's. I don't stay to read the newspapers. They'll only tell me what I heard this morning. Also, I want to be home to help Mom, so she can rest and get better.

As I walk home, I realize I've been smiling all day. Good news will do that.

I have to study history for tomorrow's test, but before that, maybe I'll listen to the radio. The Dodgers aren't playing this afternoon, but the Yankees are. They have a doubleheader against the Washington Senators. I'm not a Yankees fan, but they have some good ballplayers, DiMaggio and Dickey. The games are on the radio, so if Mom isn't listening to her soap operas, maybe I can listen to the ball games.

I greet the two old women sitting in the lobby of our building and go upstairs. I unlock the door to our apartment and hear someone crying.

Mom!

I rush to her.

Mom is in the parlor, sitting in the big chair. She's bent forward with one hand over her left eye. And she's crying.

"What is it, Mom?"

"My eye," she says through the tears. "It hurts."

"Does it hurt *that* bad?"

Mom shakes her head. It doesn't.

"But I can't see! I can't see out of that eye! I'm half blind!"

11
Another Doctor

Mom looks so weak when she's bent over like that, so vulnerable. I drop my books and just look at her. I don't know what to do next.

"I fell asleep here listening to music," Mom tells me as she sits up a bit. "When I woke up, my left eye hurt. I couldn't see out of it."

I take her hand and hold it. She starts crying again.

"You should go back to the doctor, maybe even to the hospital." Then I say, "I'm calling Dad."

The telephone is on the small table by Mom's chair, right by the radio. I lift the receiver and dial. Dad's boss answers.

"I need to speak to Mr. Duncan."

"I'm sorry. He can't come to the phone right now. He's with a customer."

"Please, tell him it's his son and it's an emergency."

What should I tell Dad? I don't know what to say, so I give Mom the receiver.

"I'm half blind," she says. "Half blind! I can't see at all out of my left eye and it hurts, but the pain is not real bad, a little like a headache. But I can't see! I can't see!"

Mom listens a bit and then gives me the receiver.

Dad tells me, "You have to take Mom to the doctor. It's just two blocks from the store. I'll meet you there."

He tells me the address.

I'm about to hang up when Dad says, "Don't take the train. Take a cab. You'll have to call for one."

I look through the telephone directory and call for a cab. Then I take both Mom's hands and pull her out of the chair. She doesn't seem to mind my help now.

As soon as we get to the stairs, Mom grabs the handrail. She walks down slowly, like an old woman, first one foot on a step, then the other, and every few steps she stops to rest. She doesn't let go of the handrail. We reach the lobby, and I take Mom's hand. The two old women are there, waiting for the mailman and talking as they do every afternoon, but when they see Mom and me, they're suddenly quiet. They watch us as we walk through the lobby.

Outside, the cab is waiting for us. We get in and I tell the driver the doctor's address.

This is my first ride in a cab. I sit in the back with Mom and watch as the price on the meter ticks up, higher and higher. When we finally get to the doctor's building, the price of the ride is eighty-five cents. Mom takes a dollar from her purse and gives it to me.

"This is for the driver," she says. "Tell him to keep the change."

"Why?"

"The rest is a tip."

I give the driver the dollar and help Mom from the cab.

Dad is standing by the curb, waiting for us. He hugs Mom. Then with one hand, he reaches around her back and holds on to her. A man in a uniform opens the door for us, and we walk into the building together.

The lobby here is not at all like ours. This one is real big, with carpeting, a large couch, chairs, mirror, and an elevator. At the far end of the lobby are two doors with doctors' names on them. Dad opens one of them and we enter a waiting room.

"Have a seat," he tells me. Then he takes Mom to a nurse sitting behind the desk. He whispers to the nurse and she leads Dad and Mom through another door.

I'm sitting at one end of a couch and a man with a bow tie, striped shirt, tweed jacket, and white mustache that curls up at the ends is sitting opposite me. He's watching me, making me uncomfortable. I take a magazine from the table, *The Saturday Evening Post*, just to have something to look at while I wait.

"Are those your parents?" the man asks me.

"Yes."

I lift the magazine in front of my face. I don't really want to talk.

"What's wrong with your mother?"

I put the magazine down and tell him, "We don't know. That's why we came here."

"Oh."

I know Mom couldn't have lost sight in an eye because she's tired. It must be something else. What's wrong? Is she going blind? She's never had trouble with her eyes. She doesn't even wear eyeglasses!

I hold my hand over my left eye and look at the magazine. I can still see. I can still read with just one eye. But if Mom lost sight in her left eye just like that, it could happen to her right eye. Then she'd be really blind. How would she shop? How would she do the laundry and prepare dinner? She wouldn't. I'd probably have to do all that—just like Beth.

"He's a good doctor," the man says. "He'll know what's wrong."

I'm not sure he's right. Just yesterday the doctor told Mom she was tired and depressed, and today she can't see out of one eye.

Blind people use long white sticks and guide dogs. If Mom can't see, she'll spend the whole day with her programs, with Helen Trent, Mary Noble, and Ma Perkins. With no one around, how will she eat her lunch? Maybe her friends Mrs. Muir and Mrs. Taylor could help.

Thinking of Mom like that upsets me.

I look up. The man is still looking at me. What's so interesting to him about a thirteen-year-old kid in a doctor's office?

The woman in the nurse's uniform returns to her desk. I go to her and whisper, "What's wrong with my mother?"

"I don't know. The doctor is examining her."

I go back to my seat and try to think of something other than Mom.

The Dodgers.

Fat Freddy is pitching tonight. It's the first night game of the year at Ebbets Field, and it's on the radio, on WOR at nine. Maybe by then we'll be home, hopefully with good news about Mom. She probably just got something in her eye and the doctor is taking it out. That's what's taking him so long.

The door behind the nurse's desk opens. Mom and Dad walk out with the doctor. Dad is holding on to Mom.

"Dr. Kellerman is waiting for you," the doctor says. "Get over there as quickly as you can."

Dad stops by the nurse's desk. He reaches into his pocket.

The doctor shakes his head. "You don't have to pay."

Of course they don't have to pay! They paid when he said mom was "just tired"! Why should they pay again when he corrects his mistake!

I follow Dad and Mom to the door.

"Good luck," says a woman who has been sitting quietly in the waiting room. The man with the mustache just watches us leave the office.

We're in the lobby of the building now and I ask Dad, "What did the doctor say? What's wrong with Mom?"

"He's not sure. He wants Mom to see another doctor, an oph . . . an oph . . ."

"An ophthalmologist," Mom says, "an eye doctor."

Once we're outside, Dad asks me to help Mom. I take her hand as he goes to the curb. He looks up and down the street and then returns to us.

"There are no cabs, and if we call one, we'll have to wait." He looks at Mom and asks, "Can you walk? It's only a few blocks."

Mom nods.

He takes Mom's arm again. I walk behind them.

Dad is usually very talkative, but not today.

Mom doesn't need help because she can't see anything, but because she's so upset. I don't blame her. I hate seeing her like this, like she can no longer do anything on her own, so I look away.

After two blocks I begin to recognize some of the stores, the Rexall Drug Store on the corner and Fancy Nancy's Dried Fruits. And there's the clothing store where Dad works.

The buildings here are nicer than the ones where we live. There are awnings leading all the way to the street, so when it rains people can get into the buildings without getting wet.

About a block from Dad's store, as we pass one

real nice building, the doorman looks at me and then quickly turns away. I think I know him, but who is he? Maybe I saw him when I visited Dad's store.

We keep walking for two more blocks until we come to the eye doctor's office. The entrance is not through the lobby. It's a bit before the awning and a few steps down. Inside, the waiting room is a lot smaller than the other doctor's office. When we step on the mat, a bell rings, and the white door opposite the entrance opens.

"Hello," the man who opened the door says. "I'm Dr. Kellerman."

He's a short, bald man. He's wearing a white doctor's jacket.

"Are you Barbara Duncan?"

"Yes," Mom answers.

"Come in."

Dad tells me to sit and wait. Then he and Mom follow the doctor.

There are magazines here, too, but I don't feel like reading them. I sit opposite the entrance and look out the window.

It's odd watching people walk by. This is a basement office, so when I look out, all I see are people's feet and legs.

A woman with shiny high-heeled brown shoes

and brown stockings passes the window, and I wonder what she looks like.

A man walks by in large workman boots and carrying a tool box. He's walking slowly, so I think either he's old or the box is real heavy.

Hey, I could probably write a story like that, about someone who lives in a basement apartment and all he sees from his window are people's feet and legs. It could be a murder mystery and the killer is caught when the main character recognizes his shoes. I bet Miss Heller would like it. I bet she'd say, "Listen to this!" lots of times.

Mom and Dad have been in there a long time.

I think again about that doorman. He had on a blue uniform jacket and blue captain's-like hat. A hat! Yes! That's who he is. It's Mr. Simmons! He doesn't wear that captain's hat and jacket at Goldman's. He must change into them when he gets to work.

Why did he turn away?

Maybe he's embarrassed that he's a doorman. After all, he told Beth and me he went to college, and he reads a lot, and he doesn't read one of those picture newspapers. He reads *The New York Times*.

At least he has a job.

I sit there, looking out the window and hope Mr. Simmons wasn't embarrassed. Dad has told me it's so hard to get a good job. Maybe that's why George is joining the navy. That's a job.

The white door opens and Mom and Dad walk out, followed by Dr. Kellerman. Dad is holding a small white card.

"Remember, you have an appointment tomorrow with Dr. Yellin. He's expecting you."

Another doctor!

When we're outside the office I ask Mom, "Does he know what's wrong with you?"

"Yes, he knows why I can't see out of one eye, but he wants another doctor to examine me."

"Why can't you see?"

"I have optic neuritis. One of the nerves in my eye is inflamed."

Dad tells me, "It's not permanent. He says it might take a few weeks, but Mom's sight will come back."

Mom should feel good that her vision will come back.

At the corner Dad says, "Let's not go straight home. Let's go to the diner. It's just a block away."

Mom seems steadier. She walks without Dad's help.

We're not in such a hurry now. Dad points to a real nice-looking building and tells us he sells suits to a man who lives in it. "Imagine," Dad says, "four suits a year, and always the best we have. He always buys shirts and ties to match, too."

Dad has just two suits. He wears them to work. And I don't have any. Dad says he'll get me one when I stop growing. Until then, it's a waste.

The diner is bigger than Goldman's, and fancier. There are framed pictures of kittens and flowers on the walls. We take a table near the front, and a waitress gives us each a menu.

The waitress is an old woman, and she takes a pencil and paper from her apron pocket and asks, "What will you have?"

Dad looks at the menu and quickly says, "Tommy, how about a hamburger on a toasted roll."

"Sure."

I look and find steak and potatoes, a roasted chicken platter, and even lamb chops on the menu. Then I see the prices and know why Dad suggested I order a hamburger. It's a lot less expensive than the other meals.

Mom and Dad order hamburgers, too.

The waitress puts the pad away. I guess she can remember our order without writing it down—three hamburgers.

Dad says, "We'll have water with that."

Mom and Dad wait quietly for the food. They both look real tired.

On the table just behind us is a young couple, and I think they're on a date.

That reminds me of Beth and our Thursday date. I think about her mother and remember she just went to two doctors. Tomorrow Mom will be going to her third.

"Mom, if this eye doctor knows what's wrong, if it's going to get better soon, why do you have to see another doctor?"

She looks at me, and for the first time I notice her left eye is a bit red.

"Dr. Kellerman doesn't know why that happened to my eye. He saw my hand shake. Then he asked me to walk around the examination room. 'You favor your right leg,' he said, and I told him my legs get stiff. That's when he said I should see this other doctor. He insisted."

"Oh."

The waitress brings us the hamburgers. There's a pickle and a few potato chips on each plate.

"I'll be right back with the water."

I lift off the top of the roll. It's a little burnt. I put it back and bite into the hamburger. The meat is red inside. I like it cooked more.

The waitress comes back with the water and asks, "How is everything?"

"Fine," Dad answers. "Thank you."

I eat slowly and drink plenty of water to wash the raw meat down. Between bites I ask Mom, "What kind of doctor is this next one?"

"Dr. Yellin is a neurologist, a nerve and muscle doctor."

I don't ask any more questions. It just doesn't sound good to me that Mom has to go to so many doctors.

12

All I Think About Is Mom

The next morning, Dad is standing by the window with a cup of coffee. He's still wearing pajamas. "The appointment is this afternoon, at two," he says without turning to me. "I could go to work this morning and come back in time to take Mom, but I'm not. I'm staying home."

I don't know what to say.

"People outside are wearing jackets," Dad tells me while I eat my breakfast. "I think it's cool out."

"Okay," I say as I get up from the table. "Good luck at the doctor," I call to Dad as I leave.

I walk real slowly down the steps and the few blocks to Goldman's. So much has happened since yesterday morning. I just hope that when I tell Beth about Mom she doesn't start talking about her mother. It's too scary to think about the two of them together.

I stop outside Goldman's and look at the newspapers on the bench. The headlines are all about the war: ALLIED SEA ESCAPE, BRITISH RETREAT REACHES COAST, and TROOPS BATTLE IN STREETS OF LILLE. Looking at them you'd think nothing is happening here in the United States.

Beth is at her regular spot. Mr. Simmons is there, too.

"It's an amazing rescue," Beth says as I come to the table. "It doesn't win the war, but without it, all might have been lost."

Now it feels good to talk about the war, especially when the other thing on my mind is so frightening.

"The rescue is like in baseball," I say, "when the other team loads the bases and no runs score. That doesn't win the game, but it can keep you from losing."

Beth smiles and says, "Yes, I guess it is."

While we talk, Mr. Simmons keeps his head down. I don't think he wants me to say I saw him yesterday, so I don't.

"Do you know how many soldiers got away?" Beth asks. "Not hundreds. Not thousands. But hundreds of thousands. They got away, but lots of them had to leave their weapons behind. We lost lots of guns and ammunition."

Beth gathers her books and newspapers. She says good-bye to Mr. Simmons and Mr. Goldman, and then, as we're walking out she asks me, "Are you ready?"

"Ready? Ready for what?"

"The history test."

"No! With everything that happened yesterday, I forgot all about it."

I tell Beth about Mom, about her eye, that she was crying when I came home, and about the two doctors.

"Today she's going to another doctor."

At the corner, I tell Sarah, too.

The traffic light is green, but we just stand there. Today, Sarah doesn't seem to mind that we may be late. I guess she knows how serious it is to have to go to three doctors in just two days. Beth and Sarah tell me it's good Mom's vision will come back and say that maybe the third doctor will know just what sort of pills Mom needs to get better. Maybe the third doctor is the one who will cure all her problems.

"Please," Beth says, "tell me if there's anything I can do to help."

Sarah touches me gently on my arm and says, "I also wish to help."

The light changes to red.

I can't imagine what Beth or Sarah can do, but it's nice they offered. Just talking to them helps.

Dr. Johnson greets us when we enter the school. He even smiles. "Good news in the papers today," he says to Beth.

In math, I open my history book to chapter twelve and hide it under my math notebook.

Mrs. Dillon is nice. She knows I understand the math and generally leaves me alone. The next period Mr. Jacobs, my science teacher, is less understanding. He walks by my desk a few times and keeps me from studying. But I do get through the two chapters, and by the time I get to history, I feel well prepared for the test.

Beth meets me at the door to Mr. Baker's room.

"Why don't you just tell him what's going on at your house. I'm sure he'll excuse you."

"I'm not a second-grader."

"What?"

"Don't you remember what he told us the first day of class, that this is not the second grade. He doesn't like excuses."

I sit in my seat and as soon as the bell rings Mr.

Baker gives his usual introduction to a test, that we should not worry, just do our best, and that our report card grade won't be based on just this one test. "I know you," he says. "I know who's been studying, who's been working."

I've been studying! I studied all through math and science.

Mr. Baker places a test on each of our desks. It's three pages of multiple-choice and short-essay questions. I take a quick look at the first few questions. Hey, I know some of these! I know *most* of these!

The multiple-choice questions are easy. Some are even funny, like this one: "Who was the oldest delegate at the Constitutional Convention? A. Franklin Delano Roosevelt; B. Babe Ruth; C. Benjamin Franklin; D. George Washington."

I wonder if anyone will choose Babe Ruth.

And the essays aren't too bad. Mr. Baker asked what we think of the Great Compromise. That's a nice way of finding out if we know what it was, but anyway, he did ask our opinions. I write that I think counting five slaves as three people seems wrong. After all, someone is either a person or not.

I finish the test with a few minutes to spare. A picture of Dad holding on to Mom flashes into my head. I stop myself from thinking about that and instead, check my answers. Then the bell rings and Mr. Baker collects our tests.

"How was it?" Beth asks me once we're in the hall.

"Okay. I think I did pretty well. And do you know what? Studying for the test during math and science kept me from worrying about Mom."

"Did you listen to the game?" Charles asks as soon as we sit at our table. "Freddy did it again!"

I forgot all about last night's game.

"Camilli made two great plays. The Dodgers won four to two."

I remember what Beth once said: "Baseball is not important." I don't really agree with her on that, but yesterday she was right. Yesterday it *wasn't* important to me.

Roger asks, "And did you listen to *The Aldrich Family*?"

I know Roger will tell us every joke, and I'm not interested. I don't really like that show, and anyway, I'm thinking about other things.

It's a few minutes after noon. Mom and Dad are probably still at home, waiting to go to the doctor. Just waiting! About now, Mom is usually at the market buying vegetables or meat for dinner, or she's cleaning the apartment. She's very particular that there be no dust, that the table, kitchen counter, and floors be clean.

"Hey, Tommy," Roger asks, "how about a game this afternoon? I already asked the others and they can all come."

"I can't."

"Why not? There's no school tomorrow. You don't have to study."

"I just can't."

The rest of the afternoon goes slowly. At three, I'm finally standing by the oak tree with Sarah. She says, "I hope the doctor gives your mother a good report."

"Thanks."

We don't talk after that, but I feel connected with her. She's worried about her aunt and uncle and other people she knows in Europe, and I'm worried about Mom.

There's Beth.

"I'll walk home with you," she tells me when she joins us.

"No. There won't be any news. I don't think Mom and Dad will be back from the doctor. The appointment was at two."

We walk quietly to the corner and after we cross the street Sarah says, "Please tell me if I can help you."

I thank Sarah again and she goes toward home.

"Don't worry and think the worst," Beth tells me as we walk. "If you ever look at a medical book you'll see how big it is. There are lots of things, problems, people get with their health, and most of them aren't serious."

We're standing in front of Goldman's. Beth takes my hand and says, "Tommy, your mother will be fine. I know she will."

Beth kisses my cheek and quickly turns and goes into Goldman's.

13

Aren't They Going to Tell Me?

The two old women are sitting in the lobby when I walk in. I greet them and go upstairs. I turn on the radio. The dial is at 570 for *The Romance of Helen Trent*. I switch it to 860, the Yankees' game against the Washington Senators. I listen for just a few minutes, until Charlie Keller hits a home run and the Yankees go ahead 1–0. Then I turn it off. Listening is boring since I really don't care who wins.

It's three thirty. By now Mom and Dad must have already seen the doctor and be on their way home. They'll want something to eat.

I go to the kitchen and check if Mom prepared dinner. Even before I open the icebox, I'm sure she hasn't. She usually does that in the afternoon, when

I get home from school. I remember we didn't have dinner at home yesterday. Maybe Mom shopped before her eye started to hurt. I check the icebox.

There's something wrapped in white paper. Chunks of meat. She probably planned to make stew, but meat is expensive. I don't want to ruin it. But with the carrots, potatoes, celery, tomatoes, and peppers Mom bought for the stew, I can make vegetable soup. I've helped Mom make that. It's easy.

I clean and cut the vegetables.

If this doctor's news is bad I might be doing this every day after school, preparing dinner and shopping, too. Maybe Beth and I can shop together.

I fill the pot a little more than halfway with water, add the vegetables, put the pot on the stove, and light the burner. The water begins to boil. I wait, then lower the flame and set the table.

It's already after four. I go into the parlor and turn on the radio. The game is in the fifth inning and the Yankees are ahead 2–0.

What's taking them so long at the doctor?

I listen to an inning and then get up and check on the soup. It smells good. I take a spoon and taste it. Mom does that. It's still a little weak, so I add a bit of salt and ground pepper. Mom does that, too.

I hear a key inserted in the lock and the door

open. It's Mom and Dad. They go right to the parlor. I follow them. Mom sits in her chair. She looks tired.

"Can I get you something?" Dad asks. "Something to drink?"

Mom shakes her head.

Dad sits in the chair next to Mom.

Aren't they going to tell me what happened?

They just sit there awhile, not talking. Mom looks up at me and smiles, but it's a weak smile.

"What did the doctor say?"

Dad answers, "He said Mom's problems, the shaking hands, her stiff legs, her eye problems, they're all because of a disease, multiple sclerosis."

"What? What's that? What's going to happen?"

Mom sighs. "We don't know. It's a problem with the nervous system. People can live a long time with it. I might be just like this for a while, with a little shaking and stiffness. That's not so bad."

"No, Mom. That's not so bad."

What else could I say?

No one talks for a minute or two.

"Now that I know what I have, I'll be more careful. I won't handle things that might drop and break."

Mom turns to Dad and says, "You know, last

week I dropped that vase we both liked."

"You liked it more than I did," Dad says. Then he turns to me. "Come on. Help me with dinner."

"But, Dad . . ."

I follow him to the kitchen and show him the soup. He tastes it and tells me it's delicious. I show him the meat chunks and he says he's in no mood for stew, and anyway, he doesn't know how to make it. He'll make noodles.

Dad takes out the noodle box and begins to read the instructions.

"I'll do it," I tell him. "It's real easy. First you boil the water. Then you pour in the noodles. Sometimes Mom adds a little salt."

While the noodles are cooking we sit by the table, and Dad tells me, "Mom may not get worse for a while. She may stay just like she is for a long time. The doctor hopes so, but he doesn't know. She may get real weak, and that could happen at any time. One day, she may have more trouble walking. She might need a wheelchair."

"Isn't there a pill she can take, something she can do to get better?"

Dad shakes his head. "He did say she should exercise, walk, even climb stairs."

"She does climb stairs. We live on the third floor."

"Yes, and as long as she can walk up and down, we'll stay here. If she can't, we'll have to move."

We sit there for a while, quiet.

Dad says, "I'll call Aunt Martha. I'm sure she'll want to know. I'm sure she'll come and visit."

She's Mom's sister. She's married, has two small children, and lives in New Jersey. I know Mom wishes she lived closer. She doesn't get to see her a lot.

Dad gets up. I turn and watch him light the flame beneath the soup pot. He takes the noodles off the stove, drains off the water, and pours them into a bowl. He opens a can of tomato sauce. Then he gets Mom and brings her to the table.

"It's good," Mom says after she's had a few spoonfuls of my soup. "Thank you for making it." She eats some more. "And don't worry," she says. "I won't get worse, not for a long time. Starting tomorrow I'll shop and cook dinner like always."

I hope she's right. I'm sure she does, too.

After dinner, Mom goes to her chair. Dad offers to help her, but she tells him she can get there by herself. Dad and I do the dishes. We don't talk. There's really nothing to say.

In bed, with nothing else to do but think, I get real upset. What can I do to help? I guess I can cook more or even bake bread. I can ask Beth for her recipe. I hope we don't have to move, and if we do, I hope it's to someplace nearby. I don't want to change schools.

The next morning when I wake up it's already after ten, but that's okay. It's Memorial Day. There's no school. I lie there and just stare at the ceiling for a while. Then, I reach down to the shelf under the small table by my bed and take *Lefty o' the Big League*, a baseball book Dad once gave me, and reread one of my favorite parts. It's after eleven when I finally get out of bed. I wash up, get dressed, and go to the kitchen. Mom and Dad are sitting at the table.

"I feel good," Mom says.

Mom's hands are on the table, folded and still. Her eye looks better, not so red. She seems relaxed.

There are a few rolls and a plate with crumb cake on the table. I guess Dad went to the bakery. I take butter and milk from the icebox and join them.

I cut a roll, spread on some butter, and bite into it.

"In a while," Dad tells me, "we're going down for a walk, maybe to the park. If you like, you can come with us. We may even go for ice cream."

Ice cream! I have a date with Beth. I have to meet her at noon.

I look at my watch. It's almost twelve. I quickly finish my roll and milk. "I have to go," I tell my parents.

"Where?" Dad asks.

"I have a—" I was about to say "date." I start again. "I said I would meet a school friend, and it's set for noon."

"Oh, then go ahead," Mom tells me, "and have a nice time."

While I'm at the sink washing my dishes, I remember I'll need money. I go to my room, open my bottom drawer, and take my wallet from its hiding place, beneath my pajamas. I open it. Two dollars. I hope that's enough.

Just then I wonder if Beth remembered our date. All yesterday, she didn't say anything about it.

As I go toward the door, Mom calls to me. "It's nice out. You don't need a jacket."

"Thanks, Mom. Bye."

This might sound wrong, but it's nice to get away. When I'm with my parents, all I think about are Mom and her illness. I shake my head as I walk toward the stairs when I realize that probably all I'll talk about when I meet Beth is just that, Mom's illness.

14

Sarah's Uncle

Beth did remember. There she is, sitting at her regular table, and even though it's not a school day, she's wearing her regular school clothes, a pretty blue dress with lots of stripes. As I walk in I feel something is different, that somehow Beth is changed, but I don't know why.

I sit across from her. She smiles. "I wasn't sure you would remember. Now tell me, what did the doctor say?"

I don't know where to begin.

"He said Mom has some nervous system disease, multiple sclerosis."

We just sit there quiet, I guess while Beth thinks of what to say, and I realize what's different. There are no newspapers on the table. I've never seen her at Goldman's, at this table, without newspapers.

Then it starts. Beth asks me lots of questions, and I do the best I can to answer them. At last, we've said all we can about it and Beth reaches her hand across the table. She takes my hand and says, "Let's get some ice cream."

I look over at Mr. Goldman sitting by the counter. He's reading a magazine.

"What flavors does he have?"

Beth laughs and whispers, "This is not one of those twenty-eight-flavor places. He has just vanilla and chocolate."

"That's fine," I say. "Even if he had lots of flavors, I'd still want chocolate."

We sit at the counter and Mr. Goldman gives us each a dish of ice cream, chocolate for me and vanilla for Beth.

I take a dollar from my wallet. Mr. Goldman waves his hand. He doesn't want to take my money.

"No," I tell him. "I want to pay for both of us."

He thanks me and takes my dollar. Beth thanks me, too. The ice cream costs ten cents a dish, twenty cents in all, so Mr. Goldman gives me lots of change.

Mr. Goldman gives himself a dish of ice cream,

too, vanilla, and then takes out jars of nuts, chocolate syrup, and maraschino cherries.

Beth says, "Let's make sundaes."

I look at the chalkboard behind the counter with the price list. Sundaes cost fifteen cents. I take two nickels from my pocket and put them on the counter. Mr. Goldman laughs, gives them back, and tells me, "A sundae is only an extra five cents if I make it. If you make it, it's still just ten cents."

I sprinkle chopped walnuts on my ice cream, pour on chocolate syrup, and top it all with a maraschino cherry.

Wow! It's delicious. I eat slowly, enjoying every spoonful, and do you know what? I didn't pay the extra money, but even if I had, it would have been worth it. If you ever have a choice of just ice cream or a sundae, take the sundae.

We sit there, eat, and talk.

Beth misses Buffalo. She had friends there and lived in a house with a garden where she planted tomatoes and carrots. She even had a bicycle. When Beth moved here, she gave it to Carol, one of her friends. "There's really no place to keep a bicycle in the Bronx, and my dad said with all the traffic it's too dangerous."

Beth pours more syrup on her ice cream.

"Carol was my best friend. Our mothers knew each other from when they were kids. When I moved, Carol said she'd write to me every week and I said I'd write to her. But we haven't. When you move, things change."

Mr. Goldman talks, too. He tells us about his two children, a son in Brooklyn and a daughter in New Jersey. They're both married and visit often, especially on holidays. His son has a son, so Mr. Goldman is a grandfather. And he has a wife and says that in the shop he prepares the food, but when he gets home, "Deborah always has a good hot meal waiting for me."

Mr. Goldman takes our empty plates to the sink and washes them. He serves a man who comes in and wants coffee and toast.

Beth suggests we go to the park.

"Not the park," I say. "Dad said he's going there with Mom and then maybe for some ice cream."

"So what. I don't mind meeting them."

Yeah, I think, so what!

We walk outside and I look at the headlines on the newspapers on the bench: DUNKIRK BOMBED! BATTLE OF FLANDERS LOST! and MILLIONS FOR TANKS, GUN, PLANES—FDR TO ASK CONGRESS.

I ask Beth, "How come you didn't read the papers today?"

"I did read them. I was here earlier. You know, I can't start the day without reading the news. Then I did some food shopping, brought it all home, and came back."

The weather is nice. We walk slowly past the bakery, turn at the corner, and go to the park. It's crowded. I guess with the holiday and nice weather, lots of people decided to go outside. I look past the open area and the swings to the benches and see my parents.

"There they are," I tell Beth, and point.

"The man with the dark hair and blue shirt and the woman in the green sweater?"

"Yes."

Beth starts toward them. I have to hurry to keep up. I guess she's anxious to meet Mom and Dad.

"Hi," she says. "I'm Beth Doyle, Tommy's friend from school. We're in the same homeroom and history class."

Dad stands, shakes Beth's hand, and says, "I'm Louis Duncan and this is my wife, Barbara."

We sit with them for just a few minutes and talk, really about nothing—you know, the weather and that the summer break from school is coming soon. At last Beth says she must get home, and I say I'll walk with her.

"They're very nice," Beth tells me when we're outside the park, "and your mom looks fine. I looked at her hands a few times and they didn't shake."

Beth looks at me, smiles, and says, "You look like your dad."

That's okay. I've heard people say he's handsome.

We walk past the bakery and Goldman's and at the corner Beth says, "Thank you for meeting me. It wasn't the celebration we'd planned, but it was nice."

"I thought I was walking you home."

She smiles and says, "Sure."

Instead of walking straight, the way I go to get to my house, we turn left and walk about three blocks. We stop in front of a building just like mine. An old man is sitting in front on a folding chair. There's a small dog on his lap.

"Hi, Beth," the man says.

"Hello, Mr. Barnett." She pets his dog and says, "Hi, Skipper."

Beth introduces me to Mr. Barnett and Skipper. "Come on," she tells Skipper and takes his paw. "Shake Tommy's hand."

I feel silly doing it, but I shake Skipper's paw.

"Hi, Beth," a young woman says as she leaves the building.

"Hey, everybody knows you."

"Not everyone," Beth says, and smiles.

We stand there for an awkward moment. Then Beth kisses me quickly on my cheek, says, "I'll see you tomorrow morning," and runs into her building.

"Sure," I say, and watch her run off. "Tomorrow morning."

Mr. Barnett tells me, "I like your friend."

"I do, too," I say, and start toward home.

■　■　■

There are just a few weeks left to the school year. I wonder what I'll be doing this summer, if I'll go to any games, if I'll see Beth. I want to.

When I get home, I turn on the radio to listen to the Dodgers games, the Memorial Day doubleheader at Ebbets Field. I shouldn't have. They're playing the New York Giants, and if there's any team I really want them to beat, it's the Giants. It's what you call a "cross-town rivalry," because both are New York teams.

The first game is depressing. Carl Hubbell is pitching for the Giants, and he gives up just one hit the entire game. He's a screwball pitcher. I don't mean he's crazy, it's just that his best pitch is the screwball. The Dodgers lose 7–0.

The second game starts out better. The score is tied in the twelfth inning, so that's not as bad as losing a one-hitter, but then the Giants score eight times. I keep listening, hoping the Dodgers will come back in their half of the inning, but they score just once and lose 12–5. What's worse is, with the two lost games, the Dodgers are no longer in first place!

Mom and Dad come home in the middle of the second game. Mom is tired. Dad tells me it's the steps. Climbing them is difficult for her.

Later, Dad helps Mom prepare dinner, and while we eat, Dad says he'll help Mom with the laundry and cleaning. The doctor said exercise would help, and Mom says, if it's okay with me, from now on when I get home from school, she'll be downstairs. "If you don't mind, you can help me shop, or just walk with me."

I say, "Of course, I don't mind," but I think about Roger and Charles and stickball. I can't play with them after school, not if Mom will be sitting in the lobby waiting for me.

"You don't have to hurry home," Mom says. "I won't leave the apartment until three fifteen, after Helen Trent."

It takes a long time for Mom to get down the stairs, so I figure she won't reach the lobby until about three thirty. That gives me time to wait for Beth after school, walk with her, even time to talk a little.

During dessert, strawberries with some powdered sugar sprinkled on them, Mom smiles and says, "Your friend Beth seems very nice."

"Yes," I say. "She is."

The next morning, when I get up, Mom is already sitting by the table. At my place is a plate with a roll, a tab of butter, and a glass of milk. Mom hadn't done that for a while, prepare my breakfast and sit with me in the morning.

"It's nice out today," Mom says. "You don't need a jacket."

"Thanks, Mom."

I guess this will be one of Mom's good days.

While I eat the roll, Mom reminds me that she'll be downstairs this afternoon, that we'll walk together and shop.

Goldman's is busy again, not like yesterday. Mr. Simmons is sitting across from Beth, and excited as usual about the war news.

"The stories that keep coming in about these men are really something," he says. "One British soldier's boat capsized and he swam seven or eight miles be-fore he was rescued."

"There are lots of great stories," Beth says, and gets up. "I'll read more of them this afternoon."

I help Beth fold her newspapers. We both say good-bye to Mr. Simmons and to Mr. Goldman and leave the coffee shop.

When we meet Sarah at the corner, I tell her what the doctor said about Mom's disease, and by the time I'm done, we're walking into school.

Sarah pats my arm, which is somehow comforting. It's always good to have friends, but especially now.

"I want to tell you some things," Sarah says. "I want to tell you what my Mutti, my mother, one day said to me. I think you should know it. I will tell you at lunch."

Sarah walks to the right and we go to the left. When we're at our lockers I ask Beth if she knows what Sarah is talking about.

"Yes, I do know, but Sarah has to tell you."

All morning, during math, science, and history classes, I wonder what Sarah's mother said, and how it relates to Mom's sickness.

At lunch, Roger goes on and on about last night's Baby Snooks show.

"Snooks was at the harbor, by the docks, and

pointed to boxes on a ship and asked what's in them. 'Cargo,' her father said. 'But where's the car?'" Roger asks in his Baby Snooks voice. "'There is no car,' her dad said. 'If the boxes were carried in a car it would be called a shipment.'"

Roger wrinkles his nose, looks up, and squeaks, "Huh!"

Roger laughs. When he sees we're not laughing he says, "Don't you get it? Things carried on a ship are cargo and things carried in a car are a shipment. It's all mixed up!"

"We got it," Charles says, and looks at me.

We both think that sometimes Roger gets too wrapped up in all his radio jokes.

Beth first looks at me and then at Sarah. They both get up, leave their empty lunch bags and waxed paper, and go to one of the empty tables in the back. Beth turns. She wants me to join them.

"I'll be right back," I tell Roger and Charles.

"Hey, what did I say?" Roger asks.

Charles tells him, "I think they want to talk in private."

Beth and Sarah are sitting on a bench near the far wall of the cafeteria. I sit opposite them.

Beth says, "Sarah wants to tell you now about her mother."

Sarah looks down, at the table, and talks. I have to lean close to hear what she's saying.

"I was born in Germany, in Frankfurt. It is a big city and very nice. We have a good apartment and many things. When I am ten, we go to Vienna, in Austria, also a big city. We must leave many things, also my books. My uncle and aunt and cousins, they moved with us. We go because of the Nazis and Hitler. It was not good for us in Germany."

"They passed many anti-Jewish laws," Beth explains.

"Yes," Sarah says. "They would not let me be in school. They did not let my Vati, my father, work. Vati is a doctor. In Vienna he took a job in a hospital. My uncle, in Germany, played violin in orchestra. In Vienna he played violin in restaurant."

I look at Roger and Charles. They are just sitting there, watching us.

"Then, when I am twelve," Sarah says, "the Nazis, they come to Austria. Mutti, my mother, says we must not keep running. We must stay. But one night soldiers with guns and papers come, bang on door, and say Uncle must go with them to play in new orchestra. That night, Mutti says she is wrong. We must go."

"Why?" I ask her. "Your uncle has a new job."

"No," Beth tells me. "They took him to play in a

labor camp. They take people all the time, prisoners, and many never come back."

I guess Beth read about that in the newspapers.

"Now tell Tommy," Beth says. "Tell him what your mother said."

"When we get ready to go, I ask, 'What about Uncle? How can we leave with him still here?' and Mutti, she says she loves Uncle. She is scared for him, but we must leave or soon they will also take us."

Sarah stops for a moment. She seems real upset.

"Yes, Mutti says, 'We go, and we go on.' She says, 'We go because we have to.'"

Beth says, "That's what my dad and I did and that's what you and your family will do now. You'll go on, because you have to."

I think about that, and I ask about Sarah's uncle. "Do you know where he is?"

Beth tells me, "Her aunt stayed in Vienna. She has gone to the Nazi headquarters, but she can't get any information. She sent her two sons here with Sarah and her family."

I shake my head. "That's awful."

"Her mom writes to her sister almost every day," Beth says, "about how the boys are, but she hardly ever gets any letters back."

"My Mutti, when she knows someone comes from

Vienna, she goes and asks if they know Aunt and Uncle, but no one does. Mutti thinks maybe they do know but do not want to say what happened."

In September, the beginning of the school year, I was so happy with my teachers, and the baseball season was getting to the exciting part, the World Series. Of course, 1939 wasn't so good for the Dodgers. So much has changed since then. So much has happened—Mom's illness, meeting Beth, the war, and now all this I found out about Sarah and her uncle. I hope things turn around, but I'm not sure they will.

15

Thank God for the Navy

After school, Sarah and I are waiting by the oak tree and Roger, Charles, Ken, Johnny, and Bruce stop by. "It's Friday," Roger says. "You can play today, can't you?"

"No. I'm sorry."

"But it's Friday. We always play on Friday."

"I know and I'm sorry. I have to help my mom with some things."

"Come on," Johnny says. "We can still play. We'll find someone else, or we'll put only two men in the field. That's fair."

I watch them walk off and hope I'll be able to play during summer break.

Beth joins us, and on the way home, we stop at

the corner for a while and talk. Sarah tells me about her two cousins. They're five and three, both boys, and don't really understand what's happening, why their parents didn't come to America with them.

Sarah shakes her head sadly and says, "I also don't understand it so much."

I ask about her father, and she tells me he's a pediatrician, a children's doctor. "He works now in hospital, in an emergency room."

If he works with children, he probably doesn't know much about multiple sclerosis.

I watch Sarah walk off with her heavy bag of books and ask Beth if it's true that in her old country people looked through school lockers.

"I'm sure it is."

"Do you think anyone looks through ours?"

"No," Beth says.

After I leave Beth off at Goldman's, I decide Dr. Johnson can look in my locker if he wants. There's nothing in it but schoolbooks and old test papers.

I open the door to our building, and there they are. The two women are sitting in the lobby, in the big cloth-covered chairs, the comfortable chairs. Mom is sitting on the steps.

"I'll put my books away," I tell Mom. "Then I'll come right down and we can walk."

"Good," she says, "and we'll go shopping. I didn't get a chance to get out earlier."

"Sure, Mom."

I hurry up the stairs and put my books away. When I get down, I help Mom from the steps. It's hard for her to get up. I want to hold on to her as we go through the lobby, but she says she can walk alone. She can, but she goes slowly. Her legs look stiff.

"Are you okay?" I ask when we're outside.

Mom nods.

"I'll be right back."

Mom nods again.

Mom leans against a car parked in front. Then I go in again, into our lobby, right up to the two old women, and say, "Please, if you can, when you see my mother, let her sit in one of the chairs."

One of the women, the heavy talkative one with short curly brown hair and lots of red face powder on her cheeks says in an angry tone, "Why? Why should we? We got here first." Then she takes a deep breath and tells me, "Do you know how old I am? Do you? I'm sixty-four years old! People should get up and let *me* sit."

The other woman, the thinner one with gray hair, asks, "Is your mother okay? She seems to have trouble walking."

"She's sick," I tell her. "She has multiple sclerosis."

"Oh," the thin woman says.

The other woman just looks at me.

I go outside, and Mom tells me, "First, I want to go to the fruit and vegetable store and get what I need to make a salad and maybe some fruit for dessert."

Mom walks slowly, so I do, too. Then she stops and tells me, "Aunt Martha called. She'll come by with John, she said, if she can get someone to watch the children."

I like her and Uncle John. He's a bus driver and loves baseball. But he's a Giants fan. He and Dad argue a lot about which team is better, the Giants or the Dodgers.

Mom stops again and says, "Isn't it a nice day." After we walk another fifteen steps or so, she stops and tells me, "I'm glad you're shopping with me. You can help me choose the best vegetables."

I don't say it, but I know she's not really stopping to tell me about the weather and how nice I am. She's stopping because she needs to rest.

The store is three blocks away, just beyond Goldman's. As we pass the coffee shop, I look in. Mr. Goldman is sitting by the counter and reading a newspaper. No one is sitting at Beth's corner table.

Mom stops in front of the fruit store. "Here it is," she says.

There's a display of apples and pears outside. We walk in, and just to the right, a man is sitting on a stool behind a counter and cash register.

"This is my son, Tommy," Mom tells him. "He's helping me."

Mom gives me a small basket to carry. Each time Mom picks up a fruit or vegetable, before she puts it in the basket, she asks me, "Tommy, does this look good?" When we're done and Mom has paid the man, we go around the corner to the grocery store.

Mom buys so much—noodles, tomato sauce, crackers, tissues, toilet paper, and other things—two full bags. She says she's buying it all for the weekend, because it's Friday, but I think she doesn't know how often she'll get out, so she's stocking up. When we're done, I combine everything into two bags. That's all I can carry.

We walk slowly back to our building. I'm getting used to Mom's many stops. Now, sometimes when she stops, she doesn't say anything. She just has her legs a bit apart, I guess for balance, and looks around as if this is the first time she's been here and she wants to see everything.

When Mom stops, I stop, too. I put the bags down. They're heavy.

"Tommy," Mom says before she opens the door to our building, "I enjoy being with you. I'm really happy you helped."

"Thanks, Mom."

One of the two women, the thin one, is in the lobby waiting for us. She's sitting, but not in one of the cloth-covered chairs. Those are empty. She's sitting on a wooden chair, the kind that folds. As soon as we walk in, she hurries to Mom, takes her hand and says, "Hello, I'm Gertrude Feiner. I live on the fourth floor."

Mom says, "I'm Barbara Duncan. This is my son, Tommy, and we live on the third floor."

"You shouldn't have to sit on the steps," Gertrude Feiner says, "and you won't if I'm here. I'll give you my seat, but if I'm not, if two other people are here, I want you to know where you can find this chair."

She folds it and says, "Follow me."

As we walk behind her she tells us, "After you left I went upstairs and got this." Now we're standing by a door just beyond the mailboxes. "I spoke with the super and he said I can keep it here."

She opens the door and puts the chair against the side wall of the closet, next to a large broom and mop.

"You're welcome to use it anytime."

"Thank you," Mom says.

"You know," Gertrude Feiner tells Mom, "I see your son every afternoon when he comes home from school and he's always very friendly. He always says hello."

Mom smiles at her and walks slowly to one of the comfortable lobby chairs. "I'm going to sit here and rest for a while," she tells me.

"I'll also sit," Gertrude Feiner says.

Mom and her new friend each sit and talk while I take up the groceries. I make two trips.

"Go ahead upstairs," Mom says when I come down for the second bag. "Gert and I want to talk awhile longer."

Good, I think. Mom has a new friend and she lives in our building, so it'll be easy for them to meet. Maybe, if Mom wants to walk when I'm at school, she can walk with Gertrude Feiner.

I open the door to our apartment and just as I am putting the bag in the kitchen, the telephone rings. I hurry to the parlor and answer it.

"Hello."

"Hello, Tommy? This is Charles."

I'm surprised. Our telephone doesn't ring much, and when it does, it's almost never for me.

"I'm sorry about the game," I say, "but I really couldn't go."

"Oh, that's okay. Johnny found another eighth-grader. He played on our team and this time we won. But that's not why I called. I called because next Friday George is signing up for the navy, and my parents are making a small party. They want me to say it's a graduation party, not a signing-up party, but that's what it really is. Anyway, it's next Friday at eight and my parents said I could invite one friend, so I'm inviting you."

"Oh, wow, thanks."

"It's not a big thing. It's in our apartment, and you don't have to bring a gift or anything, but I'd really like it if you could come."

"Sure, I'll be there."

"George says he had enough trouble just getting through high school, so he's not going to college. But he's not ready to start some boring job he'll be in for the rest of his life, and the navy should be exciting. George says he's not even afraid of fighting."

Dad says that fighting for your country can mean sitting in a muddy foxhole hoping not to be shot. I tell that to Charles, and he says his brother knows. "But George won't be in a foxhole," he says. "He'll be on a ship."

"I guess that's better," I say.

We talk for a while about that and then about baseball. He's a Yankees fan. Then I tell Charles about Mom, that I couldn't play stickball today because I had to help her shop, but I ask him not to talk about it in school, and he says he won't.

Charles is nice. He says he could help me with the shopping. "I can cook, too," he says. "I'm good at making noodles."

I laugh and say, "I am, too."

Someone is at our door so I say good-bye to Charles.

It's Mom. Mrs. Feiner is with her. Mom thanks her for walking up the stairs with her and says she'll meet her and Janet tomorrow afternoon in the lobby. I guess Janet is the other old woman's name. Then as Mom and I prepare dinner, she talks on and on about her new friend. Mrs. Feiner is a widow with a daughter who lives in Florida and two grandchildren. She visits them every winter.

Mom tells me, "She goes by train. She says she's too old to go 'in one of those flying machines.'"

"I'm not," I say. "I'd like to go in an airplane once. I don't even care where I'm going. I just want to look out of the window, look down at all the tiny people and cars."

Mom laughs. "I don't know when you'll get a chance to fly, but maybe this summer Dad and I can take you to the Empire State Building. There's an observation deck near the top. You can look down from there."

It's the tallest building in the world. It was finished just a few years ago. I think in 1931. I've always wanted to see it.

At dinner I tell my parents about the party for George.

"The navy is a good choice," Dad says. "I went over to Europe on a big boat, and after I got used to the rocking, I liked it. The sea air is so crisp and clear."

Mom says, "You'll bring a gift."

"No. Charles said it was not such a big party, that I didn't have to bring anything."

"I'm sure he said that, but still, his brother is going into the service. You'll bring him something. Dad will know what to get."

"Hm," Dad says, and thinks. "Usually something to wear is a good gift. I could buy something at the store, a shirt or tie or handkerchief, but the navy will give him all that. They'll also feed him." Dad shakes his head. "I'll have to think about this."

I think about it, too. What would I want if I was

going into the navy? A life preserver, I think, and smile. That's what I would want.

■ ■ ■

The next morning I get up late, and Dad and Mom are already out. I guess they went for a walk. After breakfast, I go out, too. I plan to listen to the Dodgers game. They're playing the Cubs in Chicago and that's in an earlier time zone, so the game doesn't begin until two forty-five. I have plenty of time. I tell myself I'm just going for a walk, but I know that's not really true. I'm going to Goldman's. Maybe Beth is there.

I get there and look in. She's not at her table. Mr. Goldman waves to me, so I walk in.

"Beth was here earlier, but just for a short while," he says. "She read a few newspapers and then went shopping."

"Oh. Could I read one of the newspapers?"

"Of course, you can. Take as many as you want, and when you're done, just fold them nicely and put them back."

I take just two newspapers from the bench outside, *The New York Times* and *Daily Mirror*.

First, I look at the front pages. It says the trapped soldiers were saved from what was sure death. The people in England went wild when they came home and lots of the soldiers shouted, "Thank God for the navy."

Well, George will be in the navy, but a different one.

I turn to the back of the *Mirror*. The Dodgers didn't play yesterday, no teams played, so there was no real baseball news. I turn to the front again. I look at both newspapers. There are more pictures in the *Mirror* and there's more news in the *Times* and at first, I'm not sure what I'm looking for. Then I realize, I want to find something about those labor camps, the ones Sarah and Beth talked about. Why would they take Sarah's uncle to play music in a camp?

But I don't find anything.

I fold the newspapers, thank Mr. Goldman, and return the papers to the bench. I want to get home in time for the game.

16

"We Shall Never Surrender!"

The Dodgers game is upsetting. The score is tied in the twelfth inning. Pee Wee Reese, our shortstop is at bat. There are two outs, and he's hit on the head by a pitched ball and taken off the field on a stretcher. He's really hurt. And do you know who takes over? The manager Leo Durocher does. He's an infielder, and once played on the Yankees with Babe Ruth. Then, at the bottom of the inning, some Cubs player hits a home run and the Dodgers lose.

Mom and Dad come home in the middle of the game, and when Reese gets injured, Dad is listening. He's as upset as I am about the game and Reese.

We get up and go to the kitchen, where Mom is beginning to prepare dinner. We offer to help, but

Mom insists we let her do it herself. She says she's having a good day and I guess, when she feels well, she wants to do things herself.

"See!" Mom says, and holds out her right hand. "It's steady. No shaking."

Mom still can't see out of her left eye, but the pain is gone and she says her legs feel better, not so stiff. She makes beef stew, with potatoes and carrots—the whole dinner in one pot. She wants to set the table, too, but Dad won't let her. I think he's afraid she'll drop one of the dishes or a glass.

"If I feel this good tomorrow," Mom says at dinner, "I want to go for another long walk. Maybe we can walk to Milly's."

Dad seems okay with that. I guess he doesn't mind walking slowly and making lots of stops.

Dad compliments Mom's stew and then tells us, "There's a program I think we should all listen to tonight. It's on WJZ at seven forty-five."

"But *Gang Busters* is on tonight. It's my favorite show."

"That starts at eight. This will be over by then. It's Senator Rush Holt talking about the war. Ben told me about it."

Ben is Dad's friend at work.

"His talk is called 'Send No American Boys to Europe.'"

With that title I don't have to listen. I already know what he'll say.

Dad and I clean up after dinner. He does the washing and I do the drying, and while I dry the pot, I wonder about Mom's good days. Will there be lots of them? And how will she feel on the days that aren't so good?

Dad tunes to WJZ early, so first we listen to a music program, and it's not swing. It's that slow stuff. Then the senator comes on.

"Shall the United States become a merchant of death?" he asks. He's almost shouting. He's not only against war. He's against having a strong army and navy. He says a well-armed United States will be more likely to fight, that it's safer to keep the army weak.

Even Dad doesn't agree with that. "If we're not prepared, it's more likely some country will attack us," Dad says. "We have to be strong and ready to fight. We always have to be ready. I just hope we don't have to go to war." Then he says quietly, "Only someone who has been in battle can know what that's like."

I'm glad when the senator's talk is done and I can tune to *Gang Busters*. I know it's a violent show, but do you know what? It's not as frightening as all this war talk.

Later, before I go to my room, Dad reminds me we're going to early mass tomorrow. He'll wake me at six thirty!

■ ■ ■

Sunday morning, after mass, Father Reilly seems very concerned about Mom. I bet Mom's friend Mildred Muir spoke to him.

Father Reilly takes both Mom's hands in his. "I'm always here for you. Please, call me during the week and tell me how you are."

Later that afternoon, we listen to the Dodgers win a doubleheader against the Chicago Cubs. Pee Wee Reese is still in the hospital, and his mother is with him. She said, "I crossed my fingers so Harold would get a hit." That's Pee Wee's real name, Harold. "He got a hit, all right!" Yes he did! He was hit on the head!

My favorite Dodger, Van Lingle Mungo, is the winning pitcher in the first game. Luke "Hot Potato" Hamlin—I don't know why they call him that—is the winning pitcher in the second game. And guess who hits the double that wins the game for Hamlin? It's Leo Durocher, the manager, who is playing for Reese.

    ■   ■   ■

It's Monday morning at Goldman's, and Beth tells me that Holt is called the "Boy Senator." He's from West Virginia and was only twenty-nine in 1934 when he was elected and had to wait a few months after his election to be sworn in. The law is you have to be thirty to be a senator.

Beth knows everything.

"Wait," I say as we leave Goldman's. "If he was just twenty-nine in 1934, he was born in 1905. He was only thirteen when the Great War ended, so he was never in any real battles."

"So?" Beth asks, and I tell her what Dad said, that only someone who was in battle could know what it's like.

"So what? Lindbergh is against us going to war and he was never in the army."

Charles Lindbergh was the first to fly across the ocean. He did it in 1927, the year I was born. He was a real hero. My dad told me there was a big parade for him when he came home. And do you know what? My friend Charles was named for him.

That's odd. Charles and his family think we should fight and the man he was named for thinks we shouldn't.

We meet Sarah at the corner, and she's more talkative now. I guess since she told me about her family, she feels more comfortable with me. She says she has something cute to tell us, something her three-year-old cousin did.

"We are listening to the news and Moshe, he looks at the radio. He goes behind it. Then he says to me, 'Where is he? Where is the man talking?'"

I laugh. It is cute. But I couldn't answer him. I don't know how sounds go through those wires. Sarah said she just told him it's a radio.

When I get home, Mom tells me that Aunt Martha visited.

"She said we should move to New Jersey. There's an apartment near her that's for rent."

New Jersey! That's a whole other state! If we moved there, I'd never see my friends.

"I told her we can't," Mom says. "Dad needs to be near his work."

And I need to be near my friends, I think. But I don't say it.

Mom is fine Monday and Tuesday. She's had a few good days, and that's great. On Monday after school, I walk with her to the fruit store. On Tuesday we go to the cleaners. Both days, when I meet her in the lobby, Gertrude Feiner is sitting on the folding chair and Mom and Janet are in the big comfortable chairs.

Wednesday morning I meet Beth at Goldman's and Mr. Simmons is at her table. He points to an open newspaper, *The New York Times*. "You've got to read this speech," he tells me. "Prime Minister Churchill is inspirational."

"I can't read it now. I have to get to school."

"He said England would fight to the death, even alone. Now, that's a leader! I just wish people here could have heard him."

"To the death," I say. "That's strong talk."

Beth closes her newspapers, says her good-byes, and tells me as we leave Goldman's, "Mr. Simmons was right. It was a powerful speech."

We meet Sarah at the corner and join the crowd of kids crossing the street and walking to school. It's a warm day. No one is wearing a jacket. Even Sarah is not in her usual long dark skirt and top. She's wearing a blue-and-white dress.

Of course, you know who's standing by the entrance to school, Dr. Johnson, but he's facing the other way. Dr. Johnson turns and sees us and smiles at me and Beth. Ever since Beth told him about the rescued soldiers, he smiles when he sees us. It's okay with me that he knows who Beth is, but I'd rather he didn't know me. I think it's bad luck for a principal to know who you are.

He asks Beth, "Did you hear about Churchill's speech?"

"I read it in the newspaper."

"It's being rebroadcast at noon, lunchtime," he tells Beth. "I'll be in my office listening with a few teachers. Why don't you bring your lunch and listen, too."

"Thank you," Beth says. "I'll be there."

"And bring your friend," Dr. Johnson says.

He means me!

I don't want to go to his office.

We walk toward our lockers and I tell Beth, "Now look what you did. I don't want to spend lunch with him and a bunch of teachers."

Beth smiles. "Please," she says, and briefly touches my hand.

That does it. I say I'll go. But all morning, through math, science, and history, I think about lunch. Eating it in Dr. Johnson's office, even with Beth, sounds to me like a punishment.

Near the end of third period Mr. Baker returns

last week's history test, the one I studied for during math and science classes. When he says he's giving the tests back, I'm afraid I failed. But he gives it to me, and I see I did pretty well.

The bell rings, and before I can leave my seat, Beth drops this note on my desk: *I'm going down the hall to tell Sarah where we'll be. She'll tell Roger and Charles. I'll meet you at the lockers.*

Roger will have fun when he hears I'm eating with Dr. Johnson. He'll joke and say I'm in trouble.

At our lockers Beth says, "Don't look so glum. Prime Minister Churchill is a terrific speaker. You'll like listening to him."

"It's not who I'll be listening to that bothers me. It's where I'll be doing the listening."

We walk together to the main office. The woman at the front desk asks us where we're going, and Beth tells her, "Dr. Johnson invited us to listen to the radio."

Behind the front desk is a frosted glass door with PRINCIPAL painted on it in gold letters. Beth opens it, and we walk in.

There are lots of three-shelf bookcases against the walls with books and photographs in frames. And on top of the bookcase right by Dr. Johnson's desk is an army helmet, the one Beth told me about. In the middle of the room is a large oval wood table with pitchers of water and juice, a stack of paper cups, and a platter of cake and cookies.

"Come in, Beth," Dr. Johnson says. Then he looks at me and asks, "What's your friend's name?"

"I'm Tommy Duncan."

Dr. Johnson reaches out and shakes my hand and says, "Hello, Tommy Duncan."

He has a strong grip. I guess he learned to shake hands that way in the army.

There are three teachers in the room, but luckily, I'm not in any of their classes. Dr. Johnson looks at the large clock on the wall and says, "I'll turn the radio on in a few minutes. The speech starts at noon."

We're all standing by the table.

"Sit down. Sit down," Dr. Johnson tells us.

Beth and I sit together, right by the army helmet. Beth takes two cups, one for each of us, and fills them with orange juice. The teachers have started to eat, so I open my lunch bag and unwrap my sandwich. Egg salad. I don't feel comfortable picking out the onion pieces, not in Dr. Johnson's office, so I just bite into it.

That's sharp! I quickly drink some juice.

The door opens and two more teachers come in,

and one is Mr. Baker. He's real friendly. Wow, am I glad I passed his test!

Dr. Johnson turns on the radio.

First, the announcer describes the scene, the British House of Commons, and Winston Churchill, who he calls rotund. Then the prime minister begins his speech.

He talks about the fighting and the trapped soldiers and says the whole of the British army "seemed about to perish upon the field." He talks about the surrender of the Belgians and how that made it harder for the British. "The enemy attacked on all sides," he says. Then he describes the rescue, how more than three hundred thousand men were saved from what he calls "the jaws of death."

I look at Dr. Johnson and the teachers. They're leaning forward and staring at the radio.

"Wars are not won by evacuations," Churchill says. "But there was a victory inside this deliverance, which should be noted."

I'm not too big on listening to speeches. No kid I know is. Well, maybe Beth. But I like the way Churchill talks, his accent. I feel good listening to him, that somehow the Allies—the good guys—can beat the Germans.

After about ten minutes or so, Churchill's voice goes up a bit. I imagine as he talks he's holding his hand up and shaking it.

He's done talking about the past. Now he tells us what to expect.

"We shall fight on beaches; we shall fight on landing grounds; we shall fight in fields, streets and hills. We shall never surrender and even if, which I do not for the moment believe, this island or a large part of it is subjugated and starving, then our empire beyond the seas armed and guarded by the British Fleet, will carry on the struggle until in God's good time the New World, with all its power and might, steps forth to the liberation and rescue of the Old."

Dr. Johnson and the teachers applaud when the speech is done, so Beth and I clap, too. They talk about the speech, and I find out that when Churchill said the New World, he meant us, the United States. He expects us to join the war. I'm sure President Roosevelt heard the speech, too, and I wonder what he thinks. Does he expect us to join the war?

I wish Dad had heard Churchill. I'm sure Senator Holt did.

The teachers eat cookies and cake as they talk. Dr. Johnson says he's sorry he's too old to sign up and fight. Then one teacher says the bell will ring soon.

He and the others get up to leave, so Beth and I get up, too.

"Don't go yet," Dr. Johnson tells us. "I want to show you something."

Once the teachers have gone, Dr. Johnson points to a framed photograph on one of the bookcases and asks us if we see anyone we know. It's a picture of a group of soldiers.

"That's you, isn't it?" I ask, and point to the young soldier on the far right of the picture.

"Yes, that's me. Do you recognize anyone else?"

Dr. Johnson was easy to pick out. I knew he would be in the picture, and Charles told me he was a sergeant, and the soldier I pointed to was clearly the one in charge. But how would I know anyone else?

Dr. Johnson smiles and points to a soldier, the second from the left, and says, "Beth, take a good look at him. Do you know who he is?"

I look at the soldier. Then I look at Beth. She shrugs.

"That's Harold Weils, your homeroom teacher," Dr. Johnson says, and laughs. "He was in my platoon."

Wow!

I take a careful look and do see some resemblance to Mr. Weils. I guess every old teacher was young once, even Mr. Weils.

The soldiers in the photograph are all standing tall, with their shoulders back, at attention, just the way Mr. Weils stands in front of our room every morning when he checks the attendance.

The bell rings. I rush to clean up my place at the table.

"You don't have to hurry," Dr. Johnson says. "I'll write you notes."

He takes a pad from his desk and writes two notes, one for me and one for Beth. We thank him and walk through the main office and into the hall.

Beth rushes off. She's anxious to get to class. I'm not. I stand there for a moment. Then I walk slowly to Miss Heller's class. Why should I hurry? I have a note from the principal.

17

A Terrible Thump

Outside after school, I join Sarah by the oak tree, and she asks, "How was Mr. Churchill's talk?"

"Great. He said the English will never surrender."

"That is very good."

"He made me feel that somehow, in the end, the Germans will be beaten."

"Yes," Sarah says. "I hope he is right and I hope soon. I hope before it is too late for some people."

She means her uncle.

Lots of kids I know walk past and wave or say hello to me. I've lived in the Bronx all my life, so I know lots of kids. But no one greets Sarah. It must be difficult moving to a new country. It was nice of Beth to become her friend, and I'm sure Sarah likes walking with us to school and sitting with us at lunch.

I look at Sarah. She's holding her leather book bag in front of her with both hands. She sees me looking at her and smiles.

"Have you heard from your aunt?" I ask.

She shakes her head and tells me, "The last letter came two weeks ago. My aunt does not know what she must do. It is difficult. The Nazis do not tell her about Uncle. She has no job. She has less money for food. People are being taken away."

"Gee, that's tough."

I think about how nice it was when Beth, Sarah, and Charles offered to help me with Mom, and I want to offer to help Sarah. But what can I do?

"Sarah," I say. "When you hear something, please let me know."

Beth comes out of school, and as we start walking I tell her I wish my dad had listened to the radio, that it would be hard for someone to be against the war after hearing Churchill.

"The speech is in this morning's newspaper," she says. "Bring it home."

Outside Goldman's, Beth takes *The World Telegram* and *Post* off the bench, both afternoon newspapers, and a morning paper, *The New York Times*. She gives me the *Times* and says, "It's in here."

I follow Beth into Goldman's and sit at her table. I open the *Times* and Churchill's whole speech is on page six. I read parts of it. Near the end he said, "We shall not flag or fail. We shall go on to the end. We shall fight in France, we shall fight on the seas and oceans, we shall fight with growing confidence and growing strength in the air."

I want Dad to read this.

I close the paper and check the price on the front. Three cents. I have that much with me. I go to the counter and pay Mr. Goldman, say good-bye to him and Beth, and walk home.

Mom is waiting for me in the lobby. Janet—I don't know her last name—and Mrs. Feiner are there, too. I say hello and hurry upstairs to drop off my books. Before I leave, I open the newspaper to Churchill's speech and put it on the table, so Dad will see it as soon as he walks in.

When I get downstairs, even Janet is friendly to me. Mom holds on to the two arms of the chair and pushes herself up. Mrs. Feiner reaches out to help her, but Mom says, "I'm okay."

I turn and look as we walk toward the door. Mrs. Feiner has folded her chair and is taking it to the closet.

When we get outside, Mom tells me she can see

a little out of her left eye. "It's a sign I'm going to get better."

I don't say anything, but as we walk, I notice Mom still walks real slow and stops a lot. But I'm glad her eye is better.

Shopping is becoming a routine for us. At the fruit and vegetable store, Mom sits in a chair by the register and tells me what we need. The clerk lets me pick what I want and I put it all in the basket. When I offer to show Mom what I chose she says she doesn't need to look.

"If you took it," she says, "I know it's good."

When I'm done, she asks me to go to the grocery store and buy a roll of waxed paper, tea, and oatmeal. "I'll wait here," she says. I leave the bag of fruits and vegetables with her and go around the corner.

We slowly walk home. At first, Mom's pace and all the stopping bothered me, but no more. I'm used to it. At one of her stops Mom says, "Martha called this morning, and so did Milly."

Now, they call almost every day, and Mom likes that. "They both said they will help me any way they can."

We enter our building, and the lobby is empty. I carry the packages upstairs while Mom goes at her own pace. She tells me not to wait.

Everything has become so difficult for her. While we were walking, she even tried to take one of the bags. I know she likes it that I help, but she would really rather do everything herself.

I'm surprised when Dad gets home. He says he listened in the store to Churchill's speech. He still hates the idea of going to war, but he doesn't know how the United States and President Roosevelt can let the Germans conquer England.

He sees the newspaper I got for him and says, "You bought me a newspaper, and I bought you a gift for George's party."

He shows me a small box and tells me it's a stationery set, nice writing paper and envelopes. "So George can write letters home."

I don't tell Dad, but paper doesn't seem to be much of a gift.

The talk at dinner begins much the same as usual. Dad asks Mom how she feels and Mom says, "This was a good day."

She always says that. I wonder if she'll ever admit she's had a bad day.

"And do you know what?" Mom asks. "Gert also listens to Helen Trent, and she reminded me about something that happened on the program a few months ago, that a man Helen dreamed of marrying turned out to already be married. He said it was a marriage in name only, that he would soon divorce his wife, but Helen said he should have told her that from the beginning. She said she could never trust him now. And do you know what else she said?"

Of course, Dad and I don't know.

"Betty, Helen's friend, asked her how she could go on after being betrayed by the man she loved, and Helen said, 'I go on because I must go on.'

"Gert told me that. She said it's something I should think about. And do you know what?" Mom says with the same determined look she must imagine Helen had. "I will go on, too, and I will do well, and not because I must, but because I want to."

Sarah's Mutti said the same thing, but I never heard Mom talk like that before. Even Dad seems surprised. My guess is Mrs. Feiner convinced her that with the right attitude she can beat her illness. I hope that's true.

"You remember," she tells Dad, "the doctor said many people with multiple sclerosis can do well for many years. I'll be one of them."

Next, I tell Mom and Dad about lunch in Dr. Johnson's office and that photograph of him and Mr. Weils. They're real interested in that. They think it's special to eat lunch with the principal and a bunch of teachers. And when they hear that Beth and I were the only kids there, they must realize we're real good friends.

"I like her," Mom says.

Of course, so do I.

While Dad and I are washing the dishes, the talk gets back to Mom's illness. "We'll help Mom," Dad says. "But remember, if she says she can do something, let her. That's important."

Dad is holding a glass.

He smiles and adds, "Just not if it's with something breakable. The doctor said her strength and coordination may not be so good."

After Dad and I clean the dishes and things, we sit by the radio and listen to the Stan Lomax sports report. The Dodgers didn't play today, but still, there's Dodgers news. Doctors say that Pee Wee Reese, the player hit on Sunday by a pitched ball, is in satisfactory condition, but he feels dizzy when he sits up. That doesn't sound satisfactory to me.

At seven thirty we tune to *Burns & Allen*. Gracie Allen is running for president on the Surprise Party and she warns all Democrats and Republicans that she has some surprises up her sleeve, along with a box of raisins.

"Raisins?" George Burns asks.

"Yes," Gracie tells him. "Sometimes campaigning for president makes me hungry."

"What about your vice president?" George asks.

"I won't have one. There won't be any vice in my administration. Remember, vote for Gracie."

I know tomorrow Roger will repeat all Gracie's jokes, and he does. At lunch on Thursday Roger is even wearing a VOTE FOR GRACIE campaign button he made from shirt cardboard and a safety pin.

Charles isn't interested in hearing Gracie jokes. He wants to talk about the war. "My dad likes what Roosevelt is doing. Dad says we have to help, and sending guns and planes to England is better than sending men."

Beth shakes her head. "They're all old guns, all from the last war. It won't be enough."

I don't say anything, but it seems to me if someone gets shot with an old gun he's just as dead as if it's with a new one.

It's odd. Outside of class all we talk about is the war, baseball, and radio. In class we're supposed to be learning what's going on in the world and we never talk about those things. It's 1940. There's a war, real history, but in Mr. Baker's history class it's 1802.

Friday afternoon Sarah and I are waiting by the oak tree. Roger and Charles stop and Roger says, "I know you can't play ball today, but will you be able to during summer break?"

"I hope so."

"Good," Roger says, and walks ahead. "We'll play in the morning, before it gets real hot."

That's what we did last summer. And most afternoons I listened to Dodgers games.

Charles lingers. "Remember tonight," he quietly tells me.

I nod. He didn't invite Roger, so he doesn't want him to know about the party. That's why he whispered, and that's why I didn't tell Beth or Sarah, because they also weren't invited.

Charles walks off and Sarah asks, "Remember what?"

"Oh, I'm just going to his apartment tonight."

On the way home Sarah asks us what there is to do here during the summer. "Mutti wants to know what she can do with the boys."

Sarah's mother feels she has to keep Yosef and Moshe busy, so they don't have time to think about their parents. It's been a while since they heard from Sarah's aunt. Sarah didn't say it, but I think they're not sure if they'll ever hear from her again.

"She can take the boys to the pool," Beth says. "It's not far away. I go there on really hot days. Lots of people do."

Beth begins to explain to Sarah where the pool is. Then she says, "I can take you there now, but first I want to check the afternoon newspapers."

Sarah walks with us to Goldman's. I look at the afternoon headlines and then walk in with Beth and Sarah. Mr. Goldman gives us a big hello, like he was waiting for us. He insists we drink something. "It's hot out," he says, and brings us each a glass of milk.

I sit with Beth and Sarah for just a short time, finish my milk, thank Mr. Goldman, and start toward home. It's Friday, and I know Mom wants to shop for the weekend.

I open the door to our building and expect to see Mom sitting in one of the comfortable chairs. But she's not there.

Mrs. Feiner rushes to me.

"Go right upstairs," she says. "You dad is here. He came home."

"Why? What happened?"

"Your mother fell. I heard a terrible thump and ran to her, and there she was on the second-floor landing, bleeding. She was coming downstairs and fell, so I called your dad."

I hurry upstairs. Mom is in her room, on her bed. Dad is with her.

"Are you okay?"

"Yes," Mom answers. "I just fell."

There are large cuts on both knees. They're bloody. Mom reaches for my hand and looks up at me. "Really," she says. "I'm fine."

I just stand there for a while. I don't know what else to do.

"Tommy, let's make dinner," Dad says. "You know how to make noodles, so that's what we'll have."

We eat at about six and it's not even four o'clock, much too early to make noodles. By dinner they'd be soggy. I follow Dad to the table. He sits, so I do, too.

Dad looks at me and says, "Mom is okay. Luckily, she wasn't badly hurt, but we can't let her walk up and down the stairs by herself. And something else."

Dad stops.

"What? What else?"

Dad looks down at the table. "We have to move. We can't stay here on the third floor."

"Move?"

"One of the things the last doctor, the neurologist, asked is about our apartment. What floor it's on. He said climbing steps might become difficult for Mom." Dad looks at me again. "Elevator buildings are too expensive. I need to find a ground-floor apartment."

I just sit there and think what all this means. If we move to a new neighborhood, I'll have to change schools. I might end up like Sarah, standing outside and no one knows me. I like my friends. I like it here.

"Mom doesn't have to go downstairs. I'll do the shopping. I'll go to the cleaners."

Dad shakes his head. "She can't be trapped here. She has to be able to get out. She'll have to go to doctors, and I can't carry her up and down."

"Is that how she got back upstairs after she fell?"

"Yes. Mrs. Feiner and I helped her up. I carried her into the apartment."

We sit there for a while. Where will we move? We've lived here for almost ten years. I like it here.

"Let's make dinner," Dad says. "We'll have noodles and salad, okay?"

"Let's make the salad now and the noodles just before dinner."

We don't have the lettuce, tomatoes, and peppers I'll need to make the salad. Dad gives me money, and before I leave for the store, I look in on Mom.

"I'm fine," she says. "This was one of my good days and I fell. That's all it was. I just fell."

"I'm going to the fruit store."

"It's Friday," Mom says. "Buy enough for the whole weekend. Get some apples and pears, and peaches if there are any. And then, if you don't mind, please get milk, eggs, and bread at the grocery."

"Sure, Mom."

I'm already doing the shopping. Soon, just like Beth, I'll probably be doing the cooking, too.

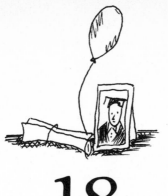

18

And I Like You

At dinner, we talk about moving and Mom says it's foolish, that she only fell this one time, and she feels good. But we all know Dad is right. Walking up and down the stairs is just too difficult. She might fall again, and the next time it might not be just a few steps—she might fall from the very top. Dad will try to find something nearby, so I can stay in the same school and shop in the same stores, and Mom can be near her friends.

I tell them I'll skip George's party, but both Mom and Dad insist I go. So, at about seven thirty I say good-bye. It's good to get out. Then I realize how Mom must feel. It would be awful if she could never leave our apartment. I'm sure she'd even get tired listening to Helen Trent, Ma Perkins, and Mary Noble.

It's a long walk to Charles's apartment, past Goldman's and about four blocks past school. It's upsetting to me to move, but it must be real upsetting to Mom. I can't imagine how awful it was for her when she fell. She had to wait for Dad, so she must have been sitting there with Mrs. Feiner for a long time. She must have felt helpless.

I enter Charles's building, and before I go up to 2D, his apartment, I walk along the halls of the ground floor and look at each door to see if there's a name on it or if the apartment is vacant. They all have names.

Lots of people probably want to live on the ground floor. It's better for shopping. You don't have to climb up the stairs carrying all those packages.

Charles lives just one flight up. I ring the bell and Mr. Jenner, Charles's father, lets me in. There are handwritten signs taped to the walls congratulating George on graduating. George is at the far side of the parlor with a few of his friends.

"Hi, George," I say, and give him the gift.

He's much bigger than Charles, but you can tell

they're brothers. They both have the same round face, small nose, curly blond hair, and quick smile.

"Thanks," George says. "Thanks a lot."

It's not such a small party. There must be twenty people here split into two groups, George and his friends and Charles with his parents and their friends. There are cakes, cookies, punch in a bowl, and sodas on the table.

Charles sees me in the middle of the room, between the two groups, and comes over.

"I'm so glad you're here. My aunts and uncles keep saying the same thing: 'I remember when you were just a baby.' Soon they'll tell me they changed my diapers!"

I laugh.

"Hey, you have to taste something. My aunt Sylvia made pinwheel cookies. They're real good."

The cookies are swirls of brown and white and they *are* good.

"Hey, what did you bring George?"

"My dad bought it. It's paper—writing paper and envelopes—so George can write letters home. Isn't that awful?"

"That's not so bad. Aunt Sylvia gave George a box of underwear, and when Dad said they give him that in the navy, Aunt Sylvia said, 'I'm sure they do, but it will be made of coarse, uncomfortable material. These are quality cotton, and anyway, you can never have too much underwear.'"

Charles tells me some of the other gifts George got—a deck of cards, a belt buckle, and a framed picture of President Roosevelt—and I think maybe paper wasn't so bad.

I tell him about Mom, that she fell, and that we'll be moving.

"That may be okay," Charles says. "You may really like your new apartment, and if you're staying in the neighborhood, you'll probably be near at least one of your friends, maybe even in the same building. Maybe you'll move into my building."

"Maybe," I say.

"You know what?" Charles laughs. "You know what Aunt Sylvia says? Don't worry about things before they happen. There'll be plenty of time to worry later."

Mr. Jenner makes a short speech about how proud he is of George. He congratulates him for graduating high school and wishes him success in the navy. He ends his talk with a salute and "Ahoy, matey!"

We all sing "For He's a Jolly Good Fellow," and then George tunes the radio to swing music.

Charles and I talk and eat cake. I'm about to take some punch, and Charles tells me not to. "Dad said we shouldn't drink it. It's got rum in it."

"It does?"

"Yeah," Charles says. "I had some when Dad and Mom weren't looking. It's funny tasting."

I drink Orange Crush. It's real cold and not at all funny tasting.

■ ■ ■

Saturday, Dad says he's tired, that we should stay home. I'm sure he is, but also, he knows Mom needs to rest. "I'll just go out," he says, "and buy some things, and then we'll listen to the radio."

Before he goes out, Dad whispers to me, "Keep an eye on Mom."

Mom and I sit by the table. She's drinking coffee, and while I do math homework, I watch her, and that seems odd to me, like she's a child and I'm her babysitter.

Dad comes back with rolls and cookies from the bakery, sodas, and a large box of Cracker Jacks. "The Dodgers game is on this afternoon," he says. "Freddy Fitzsimmons is pitching. We'll all listen and pretend we're at the ballpark."

The Dodgers are in first place again and they're

playing the team in second place, the Cincinnati Reds. At three fifteen, Dad turns on the radio. "Soda, Cracker Jacks," he calls out like the people selling that stuff call out at games. "Get your snacks here."

He gives me a soup bowl filled with Cracker Jacks. Dad and Mom are in their regular chairs. I'm sitting on the floor.

"Can you see the field?" Dad asks. "Can you see the scoreboard? Is that large post in your way?"

"I can see fine," I answer, but really, all I see is the radio.

It's all lots of fun until the game starts. The second Reds batter hits a home run. By the third inning, the Reds are winning eight to nothing.

"Dad, let's listen to something else."

We listen to music, and every ten minutes or so, Dad tunes back to the game. It doesn't get better. In the end, the Dodgers lose 23–2 and fall out of first place.

Dad had a good idea, to pretend we're at the ballpark. It just wasn't a very good game.

■　■　■

Sunday morning, I wake up and look at my clock. It's past nine. I hurry out of bed to the kitchen. Dad is there making coffee.

"What about early mass?"

"We'll go at eleven, but without Mom. It's too much for her."

At church, we sit with Mildred Muir, her husband and two daughters, and Denise Taylor. Dad tells them that Mom was just too tired to come. He also tells that to Father Reilly.

On the way home, Dad buys rolls at the bakery and a newspaper at Goldman's. I look in. The shop is mostly empty, just a man sitting by the counter, Mr. Goldman, and Beth. She's at her regular table reading newspapers.

"I'll be home soon," I tell Dad.

Dad looks in, sees Beth, and tells me not to hurry.

"Hi, Tommy," Beth says when she sees me. "The news isn't good. A German submarine torpedoed and sank a large British boat, the *Carinthia*."

I sit opposite her.

"Mom fell."

"Oh," Beth says. "Was she hurt?"

I tell her everything, including that Dad had to carry her upstairs and that we have to move.

"Have something to drink," Mr. Goldman says, and sets two glasses of cold milk on the table.

Beth tells him about Mom, and he sits with us.

"All you can do is help her," he says, "and hope for the best."

We sit there for a while, not talking. Then the man by the counter thanks Mr. Goldman and leaves.

"I'm closing early," Mr. Goldman says. "My children are coming from Brooklyn with Jacob, my grandson."

"Oh, we're ready to leave," Beth says. "I have homework to do."

"And my parents are waiting for me," I say. "I have to help Dad make lunch."

Beth and I fold the newspapers. We thank Mr. Goldman and walk outside.

Beth takes my hand and says, "I'm walking you home."

"I don't want to move," I tell her as we walk. "I like school and all my friends." I look at Beth and say, "And I like you."

She squeezes my hand. "Don't worry. Wherever you are, we'll stay in touch."

"You never write to your best friend from Buffalo, to Carol."

Beth stops.

We're in front of the cleaners. The store is closed.

Beth faces me and takes my other hand, too. She

smiles and says, "Tommy, you're more than my best friend. We'll always talk or write to each other. I promise."

Wow!

We don't talk after that. We just walk, holding hands until we get to my building. Then, just as she is about to let go of my hand, I pull her gently to me and kiss her cheek. Beth turns to me, smiles, and hurries away.

19

It Can't Be!

I t's lunchtime on Monday, and Roger wants to talk about the Dodgers and radio, the Edgar Bergen and Charlie McCarthy show, but Charles stops him.

"My brother joined the navy. He thinks we're going to war, and he wants to be ready for it."

"That's very brave of him," Beth says.

"The German Nazis are evil. That's what my dad says, and George wants to patrol the Atlantic Ocean, to keep our shores safe."

"We think they killed my uncle," Sarah says almost in a whisper. "Nazis, they took him and my aunt cannot find where he is."

"Why'd they take him? What did he do?" Roger asks.

"He just plays the violin," Sarah says, and shakes her head. "You do not know what happens there. Everyone, even children, are afraid. At night, we stayed at home. Every noise we heard, we thought it was them coming for us."

Roger says, "I don't get it."

Beth tells him, "The rest of the world is not like this country. People are persecuted for all sorts of reasons."

"Yes," I say. "When you look at a newspaper, you should look at more than just the sports pages."

As soon as I say it, I feel bad. Until just a short while ago, that's all *I* read!

That's what we talk about during lunch, the war. Sarah seems so scared, even now. Then, on the way home, she tells us she won't be in school on Wednesday and Thursday. "We have a holiday. Shavuot."

It's a Jewish holiday.

I hope her family can celebrate their Shavuot. With all that's happened to them in the last year, I'm sure it will be difficult.

When Sarah walks off, Beth takes my hand. We

walk together like that until we reach Goldman's.

"I have to go home," I tell Beth. "Maybe Mom needs me."

"I know," she says, and smiles.

She's so pretty when she smiles.

■　■　■

Mom isn't in the lobby when I get home. Maybe she needs help getting down the stairs. I go up, open the door to the apartment, and hear someone talking. It's not Mom and it's not the radio. It's a man's voice.

Dad? Why is he home? Did Mom fall?

I drop my books and hurry in.

It's not Dad's voice. It's Father Reilly!

It can't be!

The doctor said she could live a long time with her disease.

I rush through the narrow hall, past the dining table, and there is Father Reilly in the parlor. He's sitting in Dad's chair.

"Mom! You didn't . . ."

"Didn't what?" Mom asks.

She's sitting in her chair, smiling. Mrs. Muir is there, too.

"You look upset," she says. "Is something wrong?"

"No," I answer slowly. "Nothing is wrong."

What could I say? I can't tell her that when I heard Father Reilly's voice, I thought the worst.

Mom says, "Milly brought a cake. We're just about to go to the table and have some."

"Yes," Father Reilly says. "Please join us."

Father Reilly helps Mom out of her chair. He holds her arm as we walk to the dining table. The cake is round and covered with gooey-looking chocolate icing in a swirly pattern. I get the plates and forks.

"Please," Mom tells me, "boil some water for tea."

"Let me cut the cake," Father Reilly says, and takes the knife. I think he wants to be sure Mom doesn't do it.

I watch as he cuts the first piece to see what's inside. It's a yellow layer cake with chocolate cream filling. Father Reilly gives me a large slice. It's delicious.

I finally relax.

Imagine, a few minutes ago I thought Father Reilly was administering Last Rites to Mom and now I'm eating cake!

Later, at dinner, Mom talks on and on. She tells Dad about Father Reilly, what he said this afternoon and how nice it was of him to visit, and all I can think of is my horror at first hearing his voice.

■   ■   ■

Charles gave me good advice, not to worry about things before they happen. Over the next few weeks, Dad comes home lots of times and tells us about a building that has a vacancy, he thinks on the ground floor. Some are near where we live. Others aren't. Two are a few miles away and if we moved to either of them, I'd have to change schools.

I could get excited about some, because I like the building, and upset about others, but I decide to just wait.

Meanwhile, Mom isn't trapped. She goes downstairs, but only if either Dad or I can be with her. I stand next to Mom on the stairs, so if she begins to fall, I can catch her. Luckily, that doesn't happen. When she feels weak, she just stops to rest.

We go for walks together to the park, sometimes even to the stores. But really, I do the shopping. Mom makes a list of what she needs and I get it.

Near the last day of school, as we're leaving the lunchroom, I tell Roger, "My mom is sick. That's why I can't always play stickball."

"Really sick?"

I nod. "She has a disease, multiple sclerosis."

"Oh. I'm sorry."

We're standing in the hall now. Kids are rushing past us, and Roger is quiet. Then, just as I'm about to go to my class he says, "In the summer, whenever you want to play, just call me. I'll get a game together."

I thank Roger and go off to Miss Heller's class.

■ ■ ■

School finally ends, and I'm glad. I've had enough of sitting and pretending to listen to my teachers, especially when I have other things, more important things on my mind.

On the first Monday of school break, Mom asks me to go out and get a few rolls. I'm happy to go, not for the rolls, but to look in at Goldman's. I want to see if Beth is there. Well, she's at her regular table with lots of newspapers. Mr. Simmons is there, too.

"Hi, Beth."

"Hi, Tommy. Didn't anyone tell you? School is out."

I look at the headlines on her newspapers. CIG AND BEER TAX STARTS TODAY, GERMAN SOLDIERS ON BRITISH SOIL, and FRENCH WAR LOSSES, 1.5 MILLION MEN!

The war is not going well. France fell. The Germans now occupy Paris.

"When the French surrendered," Mr. Simmons says, "they had only enough ammunition for three more days of fighting."

"So now it's up to Churchill and his army," I say.

"And us," Mr. Simmons tells me. "We'll have to help the English."

"I'm going to the bakery," I tell Beth, "to get some kaiser rolls."

"Well, I'll be here awhile. I have lots to read and no hurry to finish."

That's good, I think. I really want to talk to Beth, to sit with her, but not with Mr. Simmons. By the time I get back, he should be gone.

There's a line at the bakery. Lots of people are buying bread, rolls, and bag lunches, but I feel like Beth. I'm in no hurry.

Goldman's is a bit emptier when I get back. The seats by the counter are not all taken. There are two empty tables, and Mr. Simmons is gone. I sit across from Beth.

"I spoke to Sarah," Beth says. "She heard about her aunt. So far she's safe, and she's trying to get out of Vienna."

"They got a letter?"

"Yes, from a friend, a woman who got out. She sent a letter from Turkey. They don't know where that woman is now, and they don't know anything more about her aunt, just that she's trying to get out."

"What about her uncle?"

Beth just shakes her head.

We're quiet for a minute or two. Then Beth asks about Mom, and I tell her something I've been thinking for a while.

"She seems more like my grandmother now, like an old woman who needs people, who needs me, to take care of her."

Beth says, "I felt the same way with my mom."

We sit there for a while, talk, and then go to the park. I really like being with her. And this summer I'm with her a lot.

Now that school is out, I do the family grocery shopping, and I do it with Beth. She shops for produce—fruits and vegetables—on Tuesdays and Fridays, and groceries on Mondays and Thursdays, so that's my schedule, too. I enjoy it, not the shopping part, the Beth part.

We plan to go to at least one game together, a Dodgers game at Ebbets Field. And I'm sure we will. If Beth sets her mind to do something, she usually does it.

Oh, and Pee Wee Reese, he was out for three weeks, and that first game back, he got a single, double, and triple, and the Dodgers won 10–8. And guess who pitched that day for the Dodgers—Fat Freddy Fitzsimmons.

■ ■ ■

The first week of July, George leaves for the navy. Charles knew he would, but the day he goes off is hard, so I tell him to meet me the next day at Goldman's. And as we make ice cream sundaes Charles tells me about his aunt Sylvia.

"She told George to write lots of letters home and told Mom to save them. She said when he gets back the letters will be like his diary. She even gave Mom a shoe box covered with gift wrap, to keep them in."

If he's going to write letters and save them, then paper and envelopes was a good gift.

"Aunt Sylvia came and brought cookies for George, and do you know what she said? She told George this was his chance to see the world and for the world to see him."

I tell Charles, "I never thought of it that way, that while I'm looking at the world, it's looking at me."

"Yes, Aunt Sylvia says lots of deep-thinking things like that."

"Well, my favorite is her underwear philosophy, that you can never have too much."

Charles laughs.

■ ■ ■

It's already July thirtieth, a Tuesday. Dad comes home and tells us he found a great apartment. "I didn't sign a lease. I won't until both of you see it."

The next morning we take a cab past Goldman's and the school, to an old brick building with some grass, but mostly weeds, in front.

"Before we go in," Dad says, "take a look at the block."

I look. It's not real nice. There's a building just like this one next door and then a few small stores.

"There's a fruit store," Dad says, and points, "and a small grocery, and my work is just five blocks away. I can come home for lunch."

I guess that's good.

"And do you know what? Tommy won't have to change schools."

That's *real* good!

We walk into the lobby. It's big, with a high ceiling, a few chairs, and an old but comfortable-looking couch.

Dad says, "I'll be right back. I'll get the super and he'll show you the apartment."

"The lobby is nice," Mom says, "and with the stores so nearby, I can do some of the shopping."

Dad comes back with a short, old man. He's mostly bald, and it's the middle of the summer and pretty hot, but still, he's wearing a long-sleeved flannel shirt.

"Hello," the man says, and holds out his hand for Mom. "I'm Frank."

Mom shakes his hand.

"Come, I'll show you the apartment."

We follow Frank down a hall just off the lobby to apartment 1C. He unlocks the door and we go in.

"It has a nice big kitchen," Frank says. "It's what you call an eat-in kitchen because it's big enough for a small table and some chairs."

"I can sit there and prepare dinner," Mom says.

There's a small dining area, a large parlor, and a good-sized bedroom.

"Look here," Frank says, and takes us to the two large windows in the parlor. "It's a back apartment, so it's quiet. And it has four large closets."

"I like it," Mom says.

I walk through the apartment again.

"Hey," I ask Dad, "where's my room?"

"I know. It has just one bedroom, but it's the best I could find. I thought I'd put up a curtain closing off the dining area. That could be your room."

I'll be sleeping in the dining room, right between the kitchen and the parlor. In the afternoon, when Mom listens to Helen Trent, I'll have to listen, too. I could go to my room, but really, I'll just be behind a curtain.

"If you don't like it," Dad says, "I won't take it."

Mom seems so happy with it. I look at the dining area again. It's bigger than my old bedroom.

"It's okay," I tell Dad.

What else could I say?

Dad and Mom go into Frank's apartment to sign some papers. I wait in the lobby for them and think about what this move will mean. It's not near Goldman's, so next year, I won't meet Beth there and walk with her to school. I won't meet Sarah at the corner. Maybe I could walk to school with Charles and Roger. They live nearby, but that won't be the same.

Sarah moved from one country to another. Beth moved from one city to another. Charles's brother joined the navy. This is a year of changes. I'll take Aunt Sylvia's advice. I'll wait before I decide if I like the move.

It's a long walk to the stores Beth shops at, so I'll probably just see her in school. At least I can still sit with her at lunch.

We'll talk about the war. I'm real interested in that. Well, maybe I just like talking to Beth, and since that's what she likes talking about, I do, too.

Epilogue

It's already the first Sunday of December 1941, more than a year now since we moved, and do you know what? The baseball season is over, but this afternoon, just a half hour from now, I'll be listening to a game between the Brooklyn Dodgers and the New York Giants. No, not the baseball teams. It's a game between the football Dodgers and Giants. Of course, even though it's football, I'm rooting for the Brooklyn Dodgers.

I'll always root for the Dodgers.

For the baseball Dodgers, nineteen forty wasn't their year. The team finished second, twelve games behind the Cincinnati Reds. And I didn't go to a game all summer. Beth and I wanted to, but I was just too busy with Mom, grocery shopping, and packing to move.

This year, 1941, *was* the Dodgers' year. The team finished first and played against the New York Yankees in the World Series. But the Dodgers won just one of the first three games.

The fourth game was on a Sunday, and I listened to it in Charles's apartment. He's a Yankees fan so when I cheered, he booed and when he cheered, I booed. The Dodgers were ahead until the very end. With two outs in the ninth, the Yankee Tommy Henrich struck out. That should have been it, the third out and the end of the game, but the Dodgers catcher, Mickey Owen, dropped the ball. Henrich ran to first and was safe. After that the Yankees scored four runs and won. The Yankees won the next game and the series.

Wait till next year!

When I was in Charles's apartment I saw a photograph of George in his navy uniform. He looks good. He's at a base in Virginia but Charles thinks that soon he'll be sailing to the Pacific. Charles says, when he's old enough, he's joining the navy, too.

Oh, and I'm in high school now, a freshman and I'm working harder. I try to listen in class and take notes. Homerooms are divided alphabetically, so Beth and I are still together; even our lockers are close. I see her every morning and we meet for lunch along with Sarah, Roger, and Charles. Sometimes, after school, Beth, Sarah, and I sit on a bench and talk about the fighting in Europe, and other things, including my mom. But it's not the same as meeting Beth every morning at Goldman's. I miss that.

Sometimes, on weekends and holidays, I meet Beth at Goldman's for ice cream, talk, and hand-holding. She's my girlfriend now and I wish we could meet more often, but we're both so busy.

Sarah's aunt finally got out of Vienna. She's in London, hoping to come here and be with her children, but it's not easy to get into the United States. We have quotas, Sarah says, on how many people we let in, and it depends on where they're from if we let them in, not how much they need to get out of wherever they are. Sarah's aunt doesn't know where her husband is or what happened to him. She just hopes one day he'll come back.

And Mom. It's good we moved. She walks with a cane now. Some days she really struggles, but she almost always goes out, sometimes just to sit in the lobby, but she goes out. She couldn't do that if we were in the old apartment, not with all those stairs. Also, we live so close to Dad's store that he comes home for lunch. And sleeping in the dining room isn't really so bad. It's close to the kitchen, so at night, if I wake up, it's easy to get a snack.

■　■　■

It's almost two. "Hey, Dad! It's time for the game."

Dad comes into the parlor. "Shh," he says. "Mom is resting."

He sits in his chair, turns on the radio, and tunes it to WOR. It's not really an important game. The Giants already won the division, but still, I want the Dodgers to win.

Ward Cuff—he's a Giant—kicks off and the game starts.

Dad and I aren't real football fans, but with the baseball season done, and not much else to do on a cold Sunday afternoon, we often listen to games.

Nothing happens in the first quarter. No score. Then, the broadcast stops. "We interrupt," an announcer says, "with this special bulletin. The Japanese have bombed Pearl Harbor. I repeat, we have just received word that the Japanese have bombed Pearl Harbor."

"Pearl Harbor, where is that?" I ask Dad.

"Just get your mother," he says, and turns up the volume.

"The damage is not known yet, but we do know we have definitely been hit."

I hurry to the bedroom and tell Mom, "Dad said you should come to the parlor. The Japanese bombed someplace."

"The Japanese," Mom says as I hold both her hands and help her get off the bed. "They're sided with Germany and Italy."

Mom puts her arm around my shoulder and leans on me as I walk with her to the parlor.

"We're at war," Dad tells her. "The Japanese bombed our naval base in Hawaii."

Mom holds on to both arms of her chair and slowly sits. Dad moves his chair close to the radio. I'm real close, too, on the floor, with my legs folded. Dad has tuned the radio to a news program.

"These reports are just now coming in. At Wheeler Airfield perhaps as many as one hundred P-40s and P-36s—while still on the ground—have been destroyed. B-17, B-18, and A-20 bombers at Hickam Airfield were hit, also while still on the ground. U.S. Army barracks have been bombed with a still unknown number of soldiers lost. The battle-ship *Oklahoma* was hit and is reported to be on fire. According to other reports it already sank with a still unknown loss of life."

"We're at war," Dad says.

War!

What does all this mean for our country? What does it mean for me? I'm only fifteen, too young to serve, but if the fighting lasts awhile, I might be called up. It's scary, but sitting there, listening to the reports of the attack on our men, I know I want to go, to do something.

Mrs. Roosevelt was right. The war has come to us.

Mom and Dad are holding hands. I want to talk to Beth, be with her. I call her house and her dad says, "She's at Goldman's."

It's a long way from our new apartment, past lots of buildings, stores, and my old school, West Bronx Junior High. As I walk there, the streets are eerily quiet. I guess people are inside, sitting by their radios, listening to the news.

I stand outside Goldman's and look in. It's crowded for a Sunday. I guess people came here to listen to the radio and to not be alone at a time like this. And there's Beth, her long blonde hair hanging to her shoulders, sitting on a stool by the counter.

I walk slowly to the front of the shop, and Beth sees me. We hug. There are tears in her eyes. For the rest of the afternoon we sit in Goldman's listening to the same horrible news again and again. It doesn't get better. It just feels better being with Beth.